FIZZY

DAVY BOY LAWLESS

FIZZY

Second Edition published in 2021 by Davy Boy Lawless

Copyright © Davy Boy Lawless 2021

Cover image courtesy of Glen McCourtney, Fairground Photography

Prologue

LAUGHING LIKE DRAINS

AFTER HARD WORK and diligent saving, Tom Green and I gifted ourselves with the power of flight. We bought two second-hand sports mopeds, which were built on an island nation six thousand miles away from our Leicestershire village.

It was 1977, and nothing had ever tasted so good to us

Fish and chips were like manna from Heaven; Brew X1 and Watney's Red Barrel were like nectar. We felt like we had eyes like eagles and hearing like bats. We swooped around twisty springtime 'B' roads and country lanes, racing each other like our heroes: Barry Sheene and Kenny Roberts. We pushed our bikes to the limits, broke them, and then spent happy hours in my dad's garage repairing them.

We haunted the funfairs, transport cafes, village discos, and music venues like teenage lounge lizards, looking for new sounds, tastes, or experiences. Colours had never been so vivid to us; sunsets had never been so red, nor skies so blue. And girls had never been as infuri-atingly sexy as we perceived them that summer when we were sixteen.

We never tittered or giggled coyly or politely like older people. We laughed like drains, so hard that our stomachs hurt and our faces ran with tears.

The one and only time that Tom, Trudy, and I tried cannabis, we bought an evil-smelling joint from the village hippy and smoked it at the top of the park. Then, finding ourselves strangely peckish, we wobbled down the street to the chip shop to buy some food.

At the front of a long queue, we found that none of us still had the ability to speak. The neural connections between our brains and mouths seemed to have been fogged and broken by the heady, cat piss-smelling smoke.

Desperate for chips, we leaned on the stainless-steel countertop and made idiotic, unintelligible noises at the bewildered girl behind the counter. Then we dissolved into snot-projecting, tear-inducing, uncontrollable paroxysms of teenage laughter. This laughter turned poor Trudy's legs to jelly. She collapsed in the corner of the chippy, her hands over her face, howling like a lunatic. This bizarre sight made Tom and I laugh even more. The people in the queue behind us were getting impatient, so we carried Tom's sister out of the shop, limp as a rag doll and still paralysed by hilarity. All three of us were blinded by tears of pure, golden mirth.

Though we consumed life like junkies, we didn't need drugs to make us happy. At that time, our livers were still pristine and our lungs still relatively pink. Tom and Trudy Green were my best friends in the world. We'd practically grown up together. We were closer than sardines, and I loved them both like siblings. When I was six years old, I wanted to marry Trudy and for the three of us to live in a treehouse together.

Even though kids died in summer swimming accidents in the local quarries or rode their motorbikes under lorry wheels, our village was still a safe and familiar haven. We were surrounded by friends and people who loved us. We never felt the cold or feared death. It was 1977, and we were sixteen years old. Sixteen is a magical, mystical age when you'd be most likely to see a ghost—or become one yourself.

ONE

The Road To Albarracin

THEY FOLLOWED THEIR MOTORHOME SATNAV, turned off the Autovia, and headed west on an arrow-straight road for about ten miles over flat, dreary farmland. Since retiring, Bill and his wife Sarah had been 'living the dream', touring continental Europe in their motor home. They'd read all about Albarracin on a website: 'Spain's best kept secrets'.

To the south, they saw a low range of mountains, which looked invitingly cool on the horizon, and at a place called 'Gea de Albarracin,' the road changed direction and broke through the hills, briefly heading south, giving their eyes a break from the fierce, summer afternoon sun.

They picked up the road after the village and followed the Guadalavier river valley, with ochre-coloured rocks rising steeply on their right and lush green wooded areas to their left. They had tantalising glimpses of the river through the trees. As they rounded each bend, they remarked with 'oohs' and 'ahs' at the sheer beauty of their lush, green surroundings.

Soon, the river and the road became joined at the hip. If they were lucky and observant, they glimpsed Roe deer through the trees.

They stopped at one of the many pull-ins by the river and parked in the shade. They sat on the bank and dangled their feet in the cool, crystal clear, water.

Had they been twenty years younger, they would have swam like the young Spanish family splashing around fifty yards upstream. Despite the temperature gauge reading well into the thirties, they brewed scalding hot tea in their motorhome, and sitting under the pine trees they drank it from china cups.

When faced with high temperatures and in need of refreshment, this generation of English gentlefolk often reached for the kettle rather than the fridge.

When they reached the medieval city of Albarracin, nestled in the meander of the river, they were enchanted, it was perfect and beautiful. Tall ancient buildings stained pink from the iron in the plaster rendering, rose up organically from the hillside, not a tv aerial or satellite dish to be seen. The streets were thronged with tourists and the little cave-like bars looked cool, dark and inviting.

They followed the satnav instructions to the campsite, which was within a half-mile of the town. They drove through the entrance archway bearing the sign, '*Bienvenida al* Camping Oasis, and parked in front of the smart little wood-clad reception block. The campsite had a superb rating on the website they'd looked at, and so far, they were impressed. They walked through the door and into the cool reception area.

The aircon unit purred away in the corner. Behind the counter, pinning notes to a noticeboard, was a petite, middle-aged lady with shoulder-length brown hair tied in a ponytail. She was pretty and fine-featured, with a slim, girlish figure, hazel eyes, and a ready smile.

"*Hola. Bienvenidos,*" she said.

"Hoe-lah," replied Bill, using his best evening class Spanish. "*Es possible* camping *para tres o cuatro noches*?"

"*Si,*" said the lady. "Of course," she added in English, to Bill's great relief. He and Sarah had been learning to speak 'holiday Spanish' at their local college for one evening every week. They were picking it up well, but they only had a basic knowledge of the language.

"You speak English, *señora*?"

"Yes, "she replied, smiling, "I married an Englishman. Could I have a passport, *por favor*?"

He handed it to her; "Oh, you're from Leicestershire. *Mi* 'usband is from Leicestershire," she said, dropping her Hs beautifully in the Spanish way.

As she entered their details into her computer, the couple looked around the reception. There was a glass cabinet full of local wine and olive oil for the campers to purchase and the usual rack of tourist brochures advertising local attractions. Then Bill's eyes lit on the motorbike parked to the left of the door they'd entered through. It was an early 1970s Yamaha FS1E with candy gold paintwork.

It was British registered 'M,' making it a 1973 model.

It was in immaculate condition, with gleaming paintwork and shining chrome. Every nut and bolt was perfect, and every piece of metalwork was polished to a mirror finish. Draped over the seat was a battered old leather jacket, ripped and tattered with a faded 59 club badge sewn to the arm.

"Wow! A Fizzy," Bill exclaimed. "That's a long way from home."

"Yes," said the lady, as she tapped at the keyboard. "It's *mi* 'usband's Fizzy. We love it."

"Somebody admiring my bike?" A middle-aged man appeared in the doorway behind the counter. He was slim and tanned, dressed in a Ramones T-shirt and jeans. He was carrying a canvas tool bag.

"Don't start talking about motos, Daniel. When he talks about motos, he doesn't stop," said the lady, poking her husband playfully in the ribs.

"I haven't seen one of these for years," said Bill. "They're worth a few quid now, you know. Did you ship it out here?"

"Nope," said Daniel "I rode it here."

"That's some ride," exclaimed Bill, "but I guess with breakdown cover being so good nowadays, it's all do-able. Still a heck of a good ride on a 50cc bike, though."

Daniel laughed. "I rode it here in 1977. No break-down cover, just a bag of rusty spanners and a lot of luck. I keep it here fuelled up and ready to go. If the missus kicks me out, I'm going to ride it back to Leicester," he said, grinning at his wife.

"What on earth made you ride it here in the first place?" asked Bill. "You must've just been a kid."

"I was sixteen and crazy about a Spanish girl," answered the man.

"Oh, that sounds like a good story," Sarah interjected. "You'll have to tell us."

"Don't start telling them now, Daniel, please. These people drove all day and want to go and make their camp. And you have to fix the sink in chalet three," said his wife. Turning to Bill and Sarah, she added, "The people arrive in the morning, and he's still not fixed the sink. My 'usband can talk like nobody else. If you go to the bar tonight, I'm sure he'll tell you the story. But right now, he's fixing the sink, or I'll smack him 'round the ear 'oles," she said, laughing and flicking her husband's ear.

———

That evening, in the campsite bar opposite the reception, Daniel told them his story. He'd told it countless times to curious campers who'd spotted the bike in reception. He gave them the abridged, or 'two beer version'. He was a good storyteller, and they were enchanted by it.

"Ah, that's a beautiful story," said Sarah wistfully. "So romantic. You should write a book."

TWO

Saxons-3; Normans-0

Two BOYS and a girl entered the village church. Inside, it was cool with a musty, churchy smell.

"Why do churches always smell like this?" asked the girl.

"It's the smell of the bodies rotting in the crypt," Tom told his little sister. "Anyway, keep quiet till we get into the bell tower, Trudy."

They crept down the aisle and opened the small door to the tower. Silently and in single file, they climbed the ancient sandstone staircase in the square tower. When they reached the first landing, they stopped and looked out of the unglazed slit window and over the graveyard.

"Why are the windows like this?" Trudy asked.

"It's so the Saxons could defend the church against the bloody horrible Normans," answered Daniel, the smaller of the two boys.

"The windows are long and thin, so they could fire their arrows at the attackers."

"Who were the bloody horrible Normans?" asked Trudy.

"They're what we call Frenchies nowadays," responded Daniel. "Me dad told me all about it."

The two boys both wore striped T-shirts and blue jeans with colourful snake belts around their waists. Into the belts were tucked homemade catapults. Trudy, who was maybe a year or so younger, was tomboyish with tousled brown hair. She wore shorts, and her bare legs and arms were suntanned brown from a summer of sunshine. She was also armed with a purposeful looking catapult tucked into her belt. Both boys carried brown paper potato sacks about a quarter full of small, hard crab apples.

"We're gonna get him this time, the bigger boy chimed in.

"Yep, right up the arse," replied Daniel.

They were talking about the golden weathercock on the church steeple. For weeks, they'd been trying to hit him with their air rifles, but the guns were just too puny to reach the dizzying height. Anyway, the vicar didn't take too kindly to the brandishing of weapons in his churchyard. They'd hit upon the bright idea of climbing to the battlements, which were two-thirds of the way up the tower. That way, they'd have a fair chance of hitting him right up his smug backside with crab apples fired from their catapults, or 'yackers' as the village kids called them.

They reached the final landing and stepped through the little door onto the battlements, which ran in a square around the tower. They were rewarded with a breathtaking, panoramic view of their village.

"Look," said Trudy, pointing down Church Lane. "There's our mam hanging the washing out."

Above them, the pointed spire loomed more massive than they'd ever imagined it would, and the weathercock was tantalizingly close. Daniel loosed the first shot and skimmed the top of the bird. Then Tom got a direct hit on his tail feathers and sent him spinning. Trudy proved to be a good shot as well, and pretty soon, the weathercock was spinning like a top as one hard, unripe crabapple after another scored direct hits.

The beast was conquered. No longer could he look down on the kids, smug and arrogant, as the four winds swung him gently on his axis.

Satisfied, the three walked around to the other side of the tower. They peeped through the battlements at the vicar's garden, only fifty yards away and eighty feet below them.

The party was in full swing. The vicar's favourite jazz band had been booked to play on the lawn. It was an annual event, and it was no accident that the three had chosen this day to exact their revenge on the weathercock. They knew the vicar would be busy, and the church would be empty.

"I bloody hate jazz," said Trudy.

Before the boys could stop her, she'd fired an apple down upon the peaceful scene below. It found it's mark on Mrs Taylor's tea stall, sending a couple of the church hall's green 'Beryl Ware' teacups skittering off the table.

The three ducked down behind the battlements. Thankfully, nobody had seemed to notice Trudy's attack.

Mrs Taylor fussed around, picking up the cups. She'd probably thought it was the breeze that had blown them off the table.

Trudy turned her impish face to her brother and his friend and hissed, "Bloody horrible Normans," then dissolved into laughter.

"For Christ's sake, Trudy," exclaimed her brother. "They'll see us!"

"Course they won't, Tom," she replied. "Just keep low behind the battlements."

Daniel said, "Let's just have one shot each, just for a treat, and then scarper."

"Okay, Danny," said Tom with authority. "Just one each."

They popped up from behind the sun warmed sandstone battlements, loaded, and fired. One apple thumped into the chrome tea urn with a satisfying metallic clang. Another two caused some more Beryl ware casualties.

They soon forgot all about only having one shot each. This was much too much fun. The three fired with gleeful abandon, and the vicar's tea party found itself under a full attack from the Saxons on the bell tower. Teacups were broken, tea was spilt, prettily piled rock cakes were knocked off tables, and a Victoria sponge would never be the same again.

It took the village gentlefolk a few moments to figure out where the assault was coming from, but some eagle-eyed tea drinker must have spotted one of the three ducking down between shots. The call rang out: "They're on the battlements!"

Now they were in trouble!

The vicar's garden was enclosed on three sides by a high granite stone wall, and the fourth side was the back of the Victorian red-brick vicarage itself. To catch the three kids, their pursuers would have to run down to the bottom of the vicar's long garden and orchard, through the gates, onto the street, then back up the hill to the church. That gave the kids just enough time to escape—if they were lucky.

They ran as fast as they could down the dizzying corkscrew stairway and into the cool gloom of the church. The three pelted up the aisle and burst out into the blinding sunshine just as voices could be heard close by, on the other side of the graveyard wall. They ran through the churchyard at the back of the nave and into the fields beyond. They'd been spotted, though, and they heard their pursuers close behind them. The three cleared the first field in a matter of seconds, but just as they were climbing the gate into the next one, they saw the enemy two hundred yards behind them.

"Into the cornfield," shouted Dan, and the three of them dove through a gap in the hedge.

Trudy was slowing down. "I've got the stitch," she complained.

The boys grabbed a hand each and pulled her along. The long, ripe corn whipped their legs as they ran full tilt through the field. Twenty yards in, they dropped down to the ground with the tall golden corn stalks surrounding them.

"Keep quiet!" hissed Tom. They hardly dared breathe.

Over the hedge, the three heard their pursuers.

"Must've given us the slip," said one.

"Bloody Clayford kids," said another, referring to the neighbouring village. "I'm having a word with their bobby. Tell him to keep those bloody little vandals under control."

Trudy could barely keep quiet any longer, and Tom had to hold his hand over his sister's mouth to stop her from laughing out loud. After what seemed like an age, they heard their pursuers' voices disappearing into the distance as they walked back to the vicarage. The kids crept out of the corn and ran for another three fields before they collapsed, out of breath, in the shade of a thundercloud elm. They laughed until their sides hurt and tears were running down their grimy faces.

When they thought they couldn't laugh anymore, Trudy turned to the boys, holding an imaginary teacup between her thumb and forefinger. She said with a posh accent, "More tea, vicar?"

And the three laughed even harder.

They made their way back to the village using a circuitous route through fields and along hedgerows. By the time the garden party guests were making their way home along Church Lane, the three miscreants were sitting on the park fence, looking innocent.

"Hi, Mrs Taylor," shouted Trudy from across the street. "Did you have a nice garden party?"

Mrs Taylor didn't reply. Instead, she turned to her friend and said under her breath, "She's a cheeky little minx, that one. I never quite trust her, you know."

THREE

Trudy Green, Queen Of The Scene

Every year in late May, the fair arrived on the village playing fields. First, a few smartly painted living wagons towed behind big, old post-war trucks; Fodens and Scammels, pulling rides, caravans and pay boxes in huge articulated convoys.

Snarling, grass-churning diesel tanks were driven by shirt-sleeved showmen with oily engineers' hands and an exotic air. They disembarked from their lorry cabs, dealer boots first, wearing overalls, Levis, and Trilby hats shiny with oil. With a long, cloth tape measure and a handful of wooden stakes, Joe Parker, the riding master, marked out the pitches for each beautiful, thrill-filled mechanical ride.

The showmen's wives carried their stainless-steel water jacks to the standpipe by the cricket pavilion. They filled them with water to brew tea for their Woodbine-smoking menfolk—who, by this time, were deep into negotiations regarding whose ride had the prominent position or whose sideshow was nearest the park gates. Next, more rolled thunderously and triumphantly into our village, until the whole top field of our ordinary everyday 'recky' was transformed into a travelling town.

Some of the ride owners travelled permanently with Joe Parker's 'Gaff,' often relatives, in-laws, cousins, and acquaintances. Others just joined them for single venues up and down the country. Our village 'wake' was indeed an 'awakening' for the show people, a spring solstice after the winter shutdown. We loved these people; they were like Santa Claus and the Easter bunny rolled into one.

With each new arrival, the sense of excitement amongst the village kids grew to a fever pitch. When we were little, we'd sit on the park wall waiting for them to arrive. "Here comes the Waltzer," we'd shout. Or "They've brought the Octopus this year." Our knowledge of these brightly painted trucks and their contents was quite comprehensive.

The same funfair, 'Joe Parker's Amusements On Tour,' had been coming to the village for decades. Some of the showmen's kids and 'gaff lads' who worked on the fair had become quite well known to us. The village fair was the highlight of our year. We would have forfeited our birthdays and Christmases for Joe Parker's travelling fair.

This was 1977, Jubilee year for the New Elizabethans, my best mate, Tom, and I were older now, but we still loved the fairground. The little kids went to the fair early, just after dark with their parents or grandparents, but they'd mostly all gone home by nine o'clock.

After that, village funfairs became the sole domain of us teenagers.

This year, Tom and I had motorbikes, 50cc sixteener specials. Tom had a Suzuki AP50. I, being a devoted fan of superbike champion Kenny Roberts, had bought a Yamaha FS1E, a 'Fizzy,' as we kids affectionately called them. It was like being released from gravity and given seven-league boots. We turned our throttles and were propelled into another world, magically, with noise, colour and danger, like two-wheeled fairground rides that we controlled ourselves.

We pitied people who had to walk. Putting one foot in front of the other seemed so laborious and outdated. Since we'd become motorised, we swore that we were never going to walk anywhere again.

Our house wasn't far away from the fairground—just a short walk across the big, grassy park in the centre of our community. Despite the close proximity, leather-jacketed and wearing my much-prized Bell Star helmet, I rode up the high street to the other end of the field, near the heart of our village.

I parked my bike at a place known to us kids as 'The Cross,' an area of tarmac with a couple of concrete benches near the village crossroads. There was also a wall about three feet high, which was just the right height for sitting on, and a large concrete pipe stood on its end and filled with soil where the parish council planted the village Christmas tree every December. All the local kids met here, especially in the summer. There was rarely much worth watching on the telly, and social media, mobile phones and video gaming were still decades away. If you were a village kid who didn't go 'up the Cross,' then it was probably because your parents had forbidden you from hanging around with those "louts on the crossroads."

Across the road from our meeting place was the village pub. Its only licensed competition was the working men's club down the street, with its neon CIU sign hanging over the wide granite entrance. Next door to the pub was a chip shop and café, which stayed open late in the summer serving fish, chips, and Pukka pies to the kids on the crossroads and the closing time revellers from the White Lion and the club.

The crossroads was on a tight 'S'bend, which was a great place for 'boy racers' to show off their riding prowess. With a ready-made audience of teenagers sitting at the Cross, we rode through the bends as fast as we dared, knees out, 'superbike' racing style. We missed the illuminated 'keep left' bollards by inches, sometimes millimetres. After dark, it was the ultimate 'showboat' if you could lean your bike over low enough to scrape your footrests or silencers on the tarmac and kick up an impressive shower of sparks.

Some charlatans sneakily pushed their side stands down onto the road surface when they were cornering, producing easily earned sparks and giving the impression they were riding more daringly than they were. The same kids filed their footrest rubbers to create the illusion that they'd ground them down by hard riding. Tom and I took a dim view of these people.

There were always a lot of bikes parked up at the Cross—Increasingly, more Japanese bikes than British ones. Most of the newer machines were powered by big two stroke engines, and their owners ran them on beautifully scented Castrol 'R' race oil (aftershave for bikes).

Since 1971, the British government, in an effort to discourage young people from riding motorcycles, had limited sixteen-year-olds to 50cc bikes. This had backfired gloriously though, and the Japanese and Italians had flooded the European marketplace with cheap, fast, sexy little mopeds, spawning a generation of teen petrol heads. There were usually a dozen or so of these 'pocket rockets' parked at the cross.

Most of the riders of these beautiful, noisy, liberating machines, sat on the wall, smoking, eating chips, laughing, and joking. There were always plenty of girls at the Cross as well, and a few of them even had bikes. It was a cool place to hang out. The talk amongst the boys was generally good-humoured and friendly, ribald 'piss-taking' and discussing our mutual fascination with motorbikes, music, and girls.

Occasionally, the village copper came and read us the riot act, especially if we were making a lot of noise, racing up and down the street, or having 'wheelie' competitions. When that happened, we'd decamp to one of the many transport cafes on the local 'A' roads until things had cooled down a bit. The older folks generally left us alone and didn't complain about the bikes too much. Most of them had been through the second world war and didn't mind a bit of noise. Motorbikes blasting up and down the street were far less annoying than 'Buzz Bombs' falling out of the sky. A few of them, though, couldn't stand the sight of anybody in a leather jacket and called the local police as soon as Coronation street was sullied by unsuppressed ignition leads interfering with the pictures on their Sony Trinitrons.

Friday night, first night of the fair. I lit a smoke, sat on the wall and waited for Tom. He lived just two hundred yards from the Cross, on Church Lane. I heard his Suzuki coming up the road; it sounded like a wasp trapped in a tin can. He had his sister, Trudy, helmetless, on the pillion seat.

"Lazy little mare couldn't be bothered to walk up the street," said Tom without realising the irony.

"Thanks, knobhead," replied Trudy, slapping him hard on the top of his crash helmet. "Tom's got something to ask you, Fonzie," she said to me with a big cheeky smile on her face.

"Oh, really?" I said. "What's that, Tommy boy?"

"I'll tell you later when she's gone," he replied, nodding at his sister.

She just laughed, climbed the railings, and skipped off down the park towards the bright lights and loud music of the fair.

Trudy was fifteen years old but desperate to be older. "Sixteen in June," she was quick to point out to anybody who asked. She was pretty, precocious, and confident— five feet two inches of barefaced cheekiness. She wore Levis, platform shoes, and carried a bucket bag full of makeup, cigarettes, and God only knows what else. She was an infectious, slightly dangerous catalyst. If Trudy Green had been a ghost, she would have been a poltergeist. I liked her a lot. I'd known her all my life. She was like my little sister as well as Tom's, but she could be a real handful. And despite being nearly twelve months younger than me, she teased me mercilessly.

It pissed me off when she called me 'Fonzie.' I hated *Happy Days*. Hugh Cornwall from The Stranglers had the 'look' I was trying to cultivate. My ultra-cool persona had nothing to do with Henry Winkler's limp TV impersonation of the 1950s pompadoured rocker.

Tom and I climbed the park fence and followed Trudy down the field. We could hear the music—reggae, ska, and glam rock—above the background rumble of the ex-military diesel generators parked on the fairground's perimeter. All of the rides were playing different records in a loud, discordant but exciting melee. The Maytals' "54-46" was pumping out through the Speedway's PA system. The dodgems' speakers were belting out T.Rex's "Hot Love," and somewhere in the mix, we could hear Dave and Ansell Collins's "Double Barrel."

We heard the wheels on the tracks of the Speedway, shouts, screams, sirens, and laughter. Ride operators spoke like DJs through their mics. "One way only, boys and girls. One way only," came from the dodgems. And, "Scream if you wanna go faster," came from the Waltzer.

It was a big fair this year. Alongside the Waltzer, Speedway, and Dodgems, there was a smart-looking Cyclone Twist, and Joe Parker's beautifully painted chair o' planes. There was a dozen or so stalls, a shooting gallery, a couple of 'knock 'em downs,' a penny arcade, and a lot of small rides for the little kids.

Parker's fairground was an assault on the nostrils as

well as the eyes. The smell of crushed grass, the sharp, metallic tang of electric ozone from dodgem car sparks, hot grease from fast-moving machinery, and cigarette smoke mingled with candy floss and toffee apples and the smell of onions frying on the hot dog stands. The ubiquitous, musky smell of 'Brut 33' aftershave mixed with the heady scent of 'Charlie' perfume. There was even the occasional nostalgic whiff of Pachulia oil from the few surviving village hippies who wanted their Afghan coats to smell as bad as their bedrooms.

We made our way to the Waltzer and climbed the steps to the boarded walkway. We leaned on the painted wooden railings and watched the action. Our mate "Bullshit Dave" waved and headed around the gratings to join us. We liked Dave, but as his nickname implied, he tended to exaggerate, especially where his sexual prowess or the speed of his motorbike was concerned. According to Dave, his GT 250 Suzuki could nearly break the sound barrier, and with his allegedly foot-long penis, he'd 'had' almost every girl in the village. He was quite handy in a fight, though, so nobody actually called him "Bullshit Dave" to his face. We liked him though, despite his wild and extravagant 'Walter Mitty-isms,' he made us laugh a lot.

The fairground was getting busy. There were kids from all the surrounding villages and lots of girls we hadn't seen before, which piqued our interest. We spotted our mate Sim, who was a fairground worker, a 'gaff lad.' We'd known him for a couple of years. He'd been an 'inmate' in a notoriously bad local children's home, but he'd 'ran away' when he was fourteen and found a job with the funfair. The Parkers looked after him, and he'd been given a bunk in the arcade trailer. The Parkers were good people.

Sim was from Jamaica. He was a ska and reggae aficionado, and he'd introduced us to some amazing music that we'd never heard before. The year before, he'd lent me some of his precious and rare 45s, and I'd recorded them to play on my portable cassette player. Tom, Trudy, and I had become confirmed devotees of ska, reggae, and rocksteady music. The Maytals, Dave and Ansell Collins, Jimmy Cliff, Dandy Livingstone, Desmond Decker, Phyllis Dillon—we loved them all.

Unlike most of the fairground gaff lads in their greasy jeans and sweaty T-shirts, Sim was dressed sharply in a two-tone tonic 'bum freezer' suit, with a skinny tie and black leather loafers. With his 'Pork pie' hat jammed on his head; he was every inch the 'Rude-boy.' He was fooling around on the fast-moving, rising and falling Waltzer platforms, spinning the tub shaped cars, leaning into the centre of the ride and lip-syncing to The Pioneers' "Let Your Yeah Be Yeah," which was blasting out of the PA. Every eye was on him; Sim was a natural-born showman. He usually worked on the Waltzer, sometimes the Speedway.

The Waltzer was the crown king of travelling fairground rides and every Gaff lad's favourite. Fast, furious, and always busy, it was the best ride for pulling the girls and generally showing off. Joe Parker's Waltzer was manned by a team of three: two lads walking the 'boards,' taking the money and spinning the cars, while the owner controlled the ride from the pay box in the centre.

The best Waltzer men could keep the whole ride spinning. They danced from car to car, stepping on and off the fast-moving platforms while the ride was running at high speed, casually skipping the thin line between the heavy cars full of screaming kids without ever getting 'wiped out.' It was beautiful to watch Sim and his mate Byron working the Waltzer. They were artists, 'waltzing' with the heavy, brightly painted machinery like toreadors. The boss knew that these men were worth their weight in gold, and after opening time, their job was to take the money and keep the customers entertained.

Sim saw us and waved. Seemingly defying centrifugal force and gravity, he stepped off the Waltzer and onto the slatted wooden walkway while the ride was running 'flat out,' without any effort at all.

"Bloody hell, Sim. How do you do that?" asked Tom.

"Practice, lad," Sim replied, smiling his huge, infectious smile at us. "Got some new tunes for you, Danny," he told me. "I'll play 'em later on. Got any fags?" Sim never had any smokes.

I gave him a cigarette, and we chatted for just a few seconds. Sim was working, and he didn't want to upset old man Parker. Without missing a beat, he stepped back onto the speeding ride, slipping effortlessly between spinning cars and dancing on and off the fixed platform that circled the pay box in the centre. He spun a car full of screaming girls, then jumped on the front and rode with them.

Tom and I looked at each other. "Flash git," said Tom, laughing. Sim was just about the coolest kid we knew when we were sixteen years old.

"So, what's the news, mate? What've you gotta ask me?" I said to my friend.

"I'll tell you in a minute," he replied, his eyes fixed on something at the other side of the fairground. He ran down the Waltzer's steps, towards the Speedway. I followed him, and as we stood by the fast-moving platforms, I saw what had grabbed his attention.

His sister was on the ride with her best friend Kim. They were sitting together on a painted wooden motorbike, Trudy on the front and her friend riding pillion. They were laughing and clinging to each other for dear life as the ride bucked and fell.

They were getting a lot of attention from a dodgy-looking gaff lad.

We'd met him before. He had a greasy quiff, tattoos on his wrists, and a dotted line with "*Cut here*" inked around his neck. Dressed in oily jeans and scuffed 'winklepicker' boots, he was a real sixties throwback.

He was sitting side-saddle on the bike next to the girls, leaning in close. He had his arm around Kim's shoulder, chatting them up above the din of the ride.

Tom and I didn't like this bloke. He was bad news, always perving after the younger girls. As the ride slowed, we walked around the crowded boardwalk, following the two girls on the motorbike. Tom pointed at the greaser and shouted, "Oi, mush! That's my little sister, and these girls are only fifteen, so don't get any ideas, understand?" Tom was a big lad; he had a lot of front.

The old rocker got the message. "Okay, mate. Keep your hair on. Only being friendly, that's all," he shouted back, smiling sheepishly and holding up his grimy, 'love and hate' tattooed hands.

Kim was a pretty blonde with an hourglass figure and a dazzling smile. She and Trudy were a pair of boy magnets, and Tom considered it his brotherly duty to guard their honour. Mainly, though, he was protecting his interests because he'd fancied Kim for ages. He was planning to camp out on her doorstep the night before her sixteenth birthday to ask her out.

After watching the glamorous, Kung Fu-kicking star of *The New Avengers* tv show, Trudy and Kim had converted to the 'Purdey' look, with their hair cut short and bobbed. It suited them, though they found it hard to execute flying kicks in four-inch platform shoes.

Trudy was a bit peeved with us. "Kim and I can look after ourselves. We don't need big Tom and his daft mate Fonzie watching over us like sheepdogs, anyway, if that oily git had tried it on, I'd have kicked him right in the nuts."

The sonic whoosh, pizzicato strings and tango beat of the Cockney Rebel song "Judy Teen" started playing through the Speedway's sound system. Tom, Kim, and I started singing Trudy's theme tune in unison.

"Trudy Green, the queen of the scene, she's rag doll amour."

We all laughed, even Trudy.

"So, it's *viva Espana*, then, lads," said Kim, clicking imaginary castanets over her head.

"What's she on about?" I asked Tom.

"Haven't you asked him yet, you 'paper hat'? "Mam and Dad are taking us to Spain in July," Trudy blurted out. "We can take a friend each."

"Listen, mate," said Tom enthusiastically, "all you need is some spending money. The old man's paying for the flights and hotel."

"It's gonna be brilliant, and Trudy's taking Kim," he added, turning to me with raised eyebrows and a big stupid grin on his face.

At 11:30 sharp, the rides stopped, and the hundreds of coloured lights fell dark. The generators took a well-earned break, and the gaff lads and stallholders started putting the covers and tilts on the stalls and rides. Bull-shit Dave had disappeared somewhere—probably with a pair of sixteen-year-old nymphomaniac twin sisters. Tom was walking Kim home to the other side of the village. Trudy insisted that I walked her to her door, which was only two hundred yards down the road from the park.

"You never know who's lurking in the dark. A girl's not safe on her own nowadays," she said.

She linked her arm in mine, and when we got to her gate, she turned her face to me, expecting a goodnight kiss.

"Go to bed, Trudy, I said. If your dad sees me, he'll kick my arse."

"Your loss, face ache. I'll be sixteen soon, so you'll

have to join the queue," she replied, winking theatrically and laughing. "I'd sooner kiss that greasy gaff lad anyway," she added, aiming a Purdey kick at my thigh.

I laughed and dodged it.

She walked down the drive. "Tarra, Fonzie," she called, blowing me a kiss from her front door.

I met Tom at the Cross, and we rode out to the Rendezvous café, a few miles away on the A5. This place was one of our regular hangouts. It was busy, day and night, with bikers, truckers, and weary sales reps driving Ford Cortinas and wearing crumpled 'man at C and A' suits.

The place also had a great jukebox and some excellent pinball machines. We drank tea, ate bacon rolls and chips, played pinball, and smoked. We talked about the girls we fancied, the motorbikes we wanted, and the holiday. I put some money in the jukebox and selected "Roxette" by Doctor Feelgood, and "Liquidator" by Harry J Allstars.

We were sixteen and a half years old, good-looking, with the metabolisms of racing whippets and the libidos of tomcats. We had money in our pockets, and we could shovel down junk food and copious amounts of beer with impunity. We could leap out of bed in the mornings, slide effortlessly into twenty-eight-inch waist jeans, and head off to do a hard day's work without the trace of a hangover or the addition of a millimetre to our waistlines.

Best of all, though, we were mobile.

The night was uncommonly mild for the time of year. As usual, we raced home, Barry Sheene (Suzuki) versus Kenny Roberts (Yamaha). And I'm pleased to report that on this occasion, Roberts trounced Sheenie.

I was excited beyond words at the prospect of the holiday to Spain. When I was thirteen, I'd started collecting Players cigarette vouchers. There was a two-point voucher in ten packs and a five-point one in the twenties. They were green like little Monopoly money notes. Nearly everybody I knew smoked one of the Players brands. My dad, his workmates, Tom's parents, my brother, they all saved their vouchers for me. I picked them up off the street or found them in cafe ashtrays. I even dove into a rubbish bin if I thought I could find one. It took me about six months to collect enough to get a Kodak Instamatic camera from the Players catalogue. It was brilliant. The film and developing were a bit expensive, though, so I used it sparingly.

Now that I was working, I had a bit more cash in my pocket, so I could afford to buy a couple of rolls of film for the holiday. I bought an English/Spanish pocket dictionary and phrasebook from the second-hand bookstall on our local market. I'd always liked words and language; English and French were the only subjects I'd liked at school. I poured over my phrasebook, learning some basic Spanish phrases and words.

Tom ragged me a bit. "What're you gonna say to those Spanish birds, Danny? '*Ho-lah, me Dan. I come from over wide blue ocean on big, white metal bird,*'" he said, laughing. "Listen, Danny boy. All you need to learn is, '*dos cervezas,'* for the bars and discos and, *'Hola, guapa,'* for the *chicas*."

The Greens had been to Spain the previous year. They'd stayed in Benidorm, so Tom and Trudy were annoyingly worldly about all things Spanish.

This year, though, we were going farther up the coast, closer to Barcelona, to a resort called Lloret de Mar.

"You're going to love it, Dan. There's gonna be girls everywhere, and the fags and beer are as cheap as dog meat," Tom said, using one of his dad's favourite phrases.

I'd only been out of the country twice before. The first time was in 1972, when I went with my family to the Isle Of Man to see my boyhood hero Giacomo Agostini race—and win—the senior TT. And then when I was fourteen, Tom and I went on a three-day school trip to Boulogne-sur-Mer, where all the boys in our class bought flick knives and cheap French cigarettes. We were supposed to be there to experience a bit of French culture and sharpen up our language skills, but we mostly just ran riot around the town, trying to buy beer in the bars and dodging Mr Simpson and Miss Adams, our trendy young French teachers, who were both trying to maintain a facade of innocent, platonic friendship, but were so obviously 'going at it like bunny rabbits' on the sly.

We had a trip out of town to see the Napoleon monument in Wimille, but it was a bit boring. The French had built Napoleon's column fifty-three metres high, which was exactly one metre taller than Nelson's column in Trafalgar square. I asked Miss Adams if this was because Napoleon was such a shortarse, but she told me not to be so stupid.

On the long coach trip back home to the midlands, the coach smelt horrible from the intense reek of Gitanes and Gauloises, mixed with the aroma of nasty, cheap perfume bought by some of the girls and a faint underlying smell of vomit and disinfectant.

Our glorious leaders were sitting at the front of the coach with some of the less rowdy kids. They both looked fragile, and as shell shocked as any Somme visitors in history. The trip had probably seemed like a great idea when they'd first spoke about it together in the staff room six months earlier, but now, hungover and in charge of a bus full of over-excited booze- and nicotine-charged kids, things didn't seem so rosy.

Mr Simpson stood up, cleared his throat, and faced his rowdy payload. "I must say to you all, as ambassadors for England, you lot did a pretty rotten job."

"You didn't do a great job yourself, sir," someone shouted back, and the whole bus erupted in laughter.

He and Miss Adams had got plastered on a bottle of Pastis in the hotel lobby the night before and finished up singing *"Non-Je Ne Regrette Rien"* on the top of their lungs.

That morning, though, with the prospect of a long, uncomfortable, noisy journey home and a choppy channel crossing, it was more a case of *"Oui, nous avons des regrets."*

FOUR

It's A Family Affair

THE GREENS WERE our best friends and our two families were close. On most Saturday nights in the summertime when we were children, our parents met at The White Lion, while we played in the beer garden or the park, eating crisps and drinking ginger beer.

We spent Sunday dinner together sometimes. Our mams cooking while our dads had a few pints in the pub.

There was always a fun atmosphere in the house, with music playing and the clink of wine glasses. Between peeling potatoes and making Yorkshire puddings, Sue Green and my mam were usually dancing around the kitchen.

Sue Green was a beautiful woman, five foot two, slim and pretty, with shoulder-length blonde hair cut in a fringe like Debbie Harry's. All our mates fancied Tom's mam. Sue Green was the Oscar-winning starlet of countless wet dreams. We called her the 'Dancing Queen,' and God, could she dance. When she took to the floor at family discos in the local working men's club, every male eye in the place focused on her. She made 'The Hustle' look almost obscene and watching her doing 'The Bump' with her daughter led to some serious teenage trouser embarrassments.

Tom was well sick of his mates perving over her, though, so regarding his mam, I kept my dirty juvenile thoughts to myself. She worked part-time for the family building firm in the site office, organising materials and sorting the wages. She drove a red Mini Cooper with Spitfire rondelles on the doors. Sue always looked stunning, even in wellies and a hard hat, and she was confident and cheeky with an infectious sense of humour. Considering she worked in a rough and tumble environment filled with blokes, she was never intimidated or embarrassed by the dirty jokes or slightly risqué banter that she was exposed to daily. She could give as good as she got, and the men on site loved her. It was dead easy to see where Trudy's good looks and sassy manners came from.

Sue had been working in a salon when she and her husband, Phil Green had first met, and there was an instant attraction between the pretty hairdresser and the young builder. They married soon and started their family. When they bought the old house on Church Lane, in the middle of our village, it was semi-derelict, and they both put their hearts and souls into restoring it and turning it into a beautiful home. Behind the old, white-painted Georgian walls, the Greens' place was modern and trendy. They had the first fitted kitchen in the village, central heating, a shower in the bathroom, a glass-topped G Plan coffee table in the lounge, and Tretchikoff's 'Green lady' print hanging over the fireplace.

Sue and my mam were best friends. They'd met when Tom and I were babies, at the child welfare clinic, which was held weekly in the village working men's club concert room. My mam, Sally, was a nurse and worked shifts at the Leicester General Hospital.

Sue often called in for a cup of tea and a chat with her. Sometimes, shifts allowing, they went out shopping together in the Mini, or for lunch at the local Berni Inn.

I think my mam liked to have such a glamorous, younger friend who'd order prawn cocktails, a bottle of Blue Nun, and rump steak for a midweek lunch. My mam, Sally was ten years older than her friend, she'd nursed since she'd left school at fifteen years old, though she quit temporarily when my brother Jim and I were little. She started back with her profession as soon as we'd started school. She loved her job; my mam could go on a bit sometimes, but she had a kind and caring nature.

Sue had lost her mother to cancer when she was a young girl, and I think my mam became a replacement.

Tom and I were born three months apart and grew up as close as brothers. Trudy was a year younger than Tom, and she was like a little sister to me. We'd walk into each other's houses without knocking the doors. The three of us shared our bikes, toys, sweets, and secrets, and we backed each other up like comrades in arms. We spent our childhood running wild in the fields surrounding our Leicestershire village, swimming in the quarries and rivers, and riding beat-up old mopeds along the bridleways. It was a wonderful place for children, with barns full of hay to play in, streams full of fish to catch, and no end to the mischief imaginative kids could create.

Phil Green was a builder. By 1977 Tom and I had been working weekends and holidays for a couple of years on his dad's building sites, humping hods full of bricks and mortar up the ladders to the brickies on the scaffold levels. It was hard work, but after a few weeks, it got easier. We enjoyed being on-site, having a laugh with the other lads and playing cards for pennies in the site hut when the rain stopped us from working. Phil paid us well, as he did all his workers.

After we left school at Easter, we both started working full-time on the sites. Little by little, and under the tuition of his dad and some of the other tradesmen, Tom and I both learned some building skills: how to lay bricks, trowel plaster onto walls, how to drink tea strong enough to give you palpitations, and wolf whistle at passing girls, which was a '*de rigueur*' requirement for builders in the 1970s. Along with showing up at The White Lion for 'early doors' on Fridays after work. By six pm the pub would be rammed full of men, pay packets in their pockets, having a few well-earned beers before going home and getting ready for a big night out. The flagstone floor in the bar would be thick with cement dust from work boots, and the air would be thick with smoke, bad language and laughter

Our local pub was full of characters. We had several drunkards and we had village idiots to spare. Mingling with the working-class heroes were dope peddlers, bookies runners, poachers, and fighters. And the only gay man in the village. He was one of our next-door neighbours, Chris Pinkerton, or 'Pinks' to his friends. He was our glorious village 'queen.', as flamboyant as Quentin Crisp, and the funniest man we ever knew. Parties never started until he'd arrived. He could cause near anarchy in the bar of The Lion on a Friday night and he made us laugh till we cried. We loved him. He worked in a department store in town, in the gents outfitting department, [of course]. He could have stepped straight from the set of *Are You Being Served,* and unlike our sexually ambiguous village vicar, Pinks had never spent one second in the closet. In a twist of irony, years later he became a 'lay preacher', and the Reverend Timpson hung up his cassocks and found a new career at Heathrow, [in airline hospitality].

My dad, Frank Wilbur ('Frankie' to his friends), was a carpenter, a skilled pattern maker. He was an Eastender, born near the London docklands as the Luftwaffe rained fire and destruction on the capital. Frankie was kind, generous, and resourceful. He was full of Cockney wit and charm and Trudy's number one source for slightly risqué rhyming slang.

My dad and Phil were best mates and notorious drinking partners. If they were out together 'on the ale,' there was usually a 'lock-in' guaranteed at the pub.

Frankie worked for a local firm, where there was an opening for a signwriting apprentice coming up in the following autumn. I wasn't crazy about signwriting, but my dad was keen that I got a trade behind me. I went along with the idea for the sake of a quiet life at home, but I really wanted to keep working for Phil and learn the building trade.

Working for Green's Building Contractors had enabled me to save enough money for my motorbike. I bought my Fizzy second-hand from a girl in Leicester. 'One lady owner,' the advert in *The Mercury* had read. I stumped up ninety pounds for it. Every penny was earned from humping hods or picking potatoes in muddy fields the previous autumn. It was my pride and joy—4.8 horsepower of unbridled freedom, wrapped in gorgeous candy gold metallic paint.

Tom and I had stuck together all through high school and later the Comprehensive in the nearby town. Though we were in different classes, we'd meet up at break times. We wagged the day off school to get matching tattoos at a place on Filbert street near the Leicester City football ground. Stylised, multicoloured swallows flying across our forearms for three quid each —which we considered a bargain because tattoos were handy. Along with embryonic moustaches and builders' muscles, they gave landlords and landladies the impression that we were old enough to be in a bar.

When we were just fifteen years old, we stuffed our school blazers into a hedge, rolled up our sleeves, and flashing our new tattoos we walked into a pub in town. Due to some diligent facial hair cultivation over the previous weeks, we easily convinced the barmaid that we were old enough to buy beer. We were two pints into our school dinner break, leaning on the bar, smoking and swigging beer like old hands. Tom was in the process of persuading the twenty-year-old barmaid to go out on a date with him when, to our horror, we saw McReynolds, our borderline psycho PE teacher, walk through the front door. Rather than leave our half-finished beers, we slipped out the back and finished our drinks in the yard before climbing the wall and escaping.

"Bollocks! Another five minutes and I would've had her," Tom remonstrated as we walked the half-mile back to double maths and French.

We were fifteen, going on twenty.

At the weekends and holidays, we'd be humping hods full of bricks up ladders with the rest of the guys. Then from Monday to Friday, we were school kids again, being told what to do by some windy old fart or being harangued for not doing our homework.

It was confusing. We hated being in school, and we were always in trouble.

Neither one of us was sad to see the end of our school days. On our last day, we cut each other's ties in half, let the air out of the deputy head's car tyres, changed into our civvies, and walked downtown for a celebratory pint.

· ı

FIVE

Blitzkrieg Bop

EVER SINCE TOM and I saw The Ramones on Top of the Pops and heard 'Sheena is a Punk Rocker,' we were dedicated fans.

We bought beat up Brando-style leather jackets, tight jeans, and baseball boots. Unless it was freezing, we only ever wore T-shirts under our leathers. After all the hard graft that we'd done shovelling mortar and carrying hods, I've got to admit, we both looked good. Tom took after his dad; he was big, a couple of inches taller than me, well-built. Like me, he'd benefited from the hard work on the building site. He was good looking with a mop of brown hair which he wore long, Dee Dee Ramone style. I wore my hair shorter with a quiff, like Hugh Cornwall from The Stranglers. I liked it like that, even though Trudy called me Fonzie and Sue said I looked like Tony Curtis.

Tom and I had an eclectic taste in music. We loved punk, rocksteady, ska, northern soul, 1960s beat bands, and even glam rock and disco.

The fortnightly village disco attracted kids from all the neighbouring villages. It was nothing special, just a big, old, draughty church hall with a high wooden stage where the mobile DJ setup with his decks, sound system, and lights. But when the place was rammed full of teenagers, dancing, laughing, boys and girls eyeing each other up through the smoke-layered atmosphere, huge speakers blasting out our favourite songs, condensation running down the walls, and lust and longing hanging in the air like incense. Then the dreary old Methodist hall became a fortnightly magical maelstrom of teenage emotion and sexual tension, unrequited love, and clumsy romance. The place was wonderful and as funky as hell.

The DJ had his work cut out. There was a diverse mix of tribes in the venue: soul boys, rude boys, plastic teds, skins, suede heads, mods, and rockers (though these last two were getting a bit thin on the ground). There was also a growing number of weekend punks with ripped T-shirts, bondage trousers, and fake safety pins in their cheeks.

Tom and I got there at about 8:30. We were going to check out the talent and then head down to the fair later. After pulling a few wheelies in the car park for the benefit of a group of girls standing by the door, we parked our 'peds' in the row of bikes, paid our thirty pence to the old girl working the door, and walked in, each with a can of Red Stripe lager hidden inside our crash helmets. It was soft drinks only at the Methodist Hall, so some of us older kids smuggled in a beer or two and drank it discreetly. Though, there was always the risk of being thrown out if you were caught or, even worse, banned from the social highlight of the village calendar.

The ancient Methodist hall had been used for dances since the 1950s. The old folks used to call it 'the temperance hop' because of the no-alcohol rule, but the youths of 1977 were a bit thirstier than their parents had been.

The DJ was playing "Blitzkrieg Bop" by the Ramones. Tom and I put our helmets down on the front of the stage and joined the melee pogoing on the dance-floor. The Pogo was a dance that could have been invented for me. It was easy; all you had to do was jump up and down. Anything else was optional, which was handy because I didn't have many more moves. Unlike Tom, I was never a demon on the dance floor. Even Trudy was reluctant to dance with me, unless it was a slow song or rocksteady (Sim had taught me how to dance to ska). Trudy said that I looked like I was trying to wipe dog shit off my shoes when I danced. She had a wonderful way with words.

It was 1977, and punk rock was hitting its stride. There was a new wave of exciting, hard-edged bands headbanging their way through the mediocrity of the British pop charts. ABBA and Barry White were still filling the dancefloor at our village disco, but they were interspersed by three-minute blasts of The Stranglers, The Ramones, The Jam, and other groups that had emerged from the London pub circuit like Doctor Feel-good and Ian Dury and The Blockheads. Watching these urgent, amphetamine-driven rockers on top of the pops in 1977 was like seeing axe men running wild in a nursing home.

Kim and Trudy were dancing around their hand-bags to Tavares' "Heaven Must Be Missing an Angel" when some youths from the local town, whom we knew from our school days, started fooling around with them. They were dancing close behind the girls, groping them and holding them around their waists. These boys were seventeen- and eighteen-year-olds, and they were always trouble. They'd get tanked up in the pubs in town, and then head out to the village for the disco.

One of them, a 'weekend skinhead' wearing white 'Skinner' jeans and Doc Marten boots, was an old school adversary of Tom's. They'd had a fight in the school gym a few years earlier, and despite being in the year below, Tom had held his ground. Since then, they'd given each other a wide berth.

Trudy and Kim had already turned around and given the youths a mouthful. It had probably started out as a bit of fun, but now the girls were looking uncom-fortable. Tom and I watched for a minute. We saw his sister scanning the people on the edge of the dance floor, looking for us. Without a word to each other, we pushed our way through the dancers and made a beeline for the youths.

Tom grabbed his old sparring partner by the collar of his Levi jacket and yanked him hard backwards. He fell heavily, right on his backside on the dancefloor. Tom slapped him with the flat of his hand, full force on his right ear. The guy didn't know what had hit him, and he held his hand over his ringing ear in obvious agony. His friend turned around to see what was happening, and I punched him square on the nose before he could do anything. He tried to fight back, but his eyes were watering so much, he just flailed his arms wildly and staggered around. The third youth decided against trying his luck and melted away into the crowd.

The lights came on, the music stopped, and the four of us were pushed out of the door by the 'Methodist militia,' as we called the disco security, which consisted of some village cricket team old boys and the local youth club leader. Tom and I held our hands up and went peacefully. A bit of a scuffle continued in the car park, watched by an audience that had followed the commotion out of the hall. We got the better of them again, and they sloped off towards the bus stop to jeers and a bit of choice language from Tom and me.

Trudy and Kim were standing close by. They'd picked our helmets up and followed us out of the hall, and now they were remonstrating with the Methodist bouncers, telling them that it wasn't mine and Tom's fault. We'd only been looking after them.

Their pleas were falling on deaf ears, though.

"Give it up, girls," I said. "Let's go to the fair."

Sim was working the Waltzer again that night. Ten minutes later, we were all standing on the boardwalk, telling him and Bullshit Dave all about the fight. Our few wild punches had been embellished a little bit as we retold the story, but it was nearly all true.

. . .

The Waltzer's sound system was thumping out "Shanty-town" by Desmond Dekker, and the place was getting busy. A lot of kids had left the disco early to come down to the fair. We thought we'd stick around and make the most of our newfound hero status.

Kim was gazing slightly starry-eyed at Tom as he milked the situation and re-enacted his eardrum bursting slap. Trudy had been uncharacteristically quiet since we'd left the disco. I supposed we'd be barred for a few weeks, but we didn't have any choice. We couldn't have stood by and watched Tom's little sister and her mate getting abuse from those Neanderthals.

The night was warm for May, and Tom and I would probably ride out to the Rendezvous later. I supposed I ought to give Sheenie a chance for a rematch, or maybe we'd take our 'L' plates off and take the girls with us. There shouldn't be many coppers around later, and we could take the back roads.

We all climbed into a Waltzer car, and Sim spun us until we were nearly sick. I was sitting at the opposite end of the car to Trudy. I watched her as the car spun fast on the rails. She was holding on to Kim and laughing out loud. Her hair was flying about behind her, and her eyes were bright and shining under the hundreds of coloured light bulbs. I hadn't really noticed until then how pretty she was, and despite the constant ribbing she gave me, I liked her a lot.

SIX

Drinking Homebrew and Skanking

THE FAIR NEVER OPENED ON Sunday nights, so Sim and Tom came to our house for dinner. Tom usually spent half of his life around at our house anyway. He loved my mam's Yorkshire puddings, so if our two families weren't eating together, then he'd often turn up (coincidentally) around dinnertime on a Sunday. As for Sim, my parents were fond of him. He knocked on our back door at noon, dressed smart in his full 'Rudeboy' suit, pork pie hat on his head and carrying a Woolies plastic carrier bag full of singles and some flowers for my mam.

"Mam, Sim's been down the graveyard again, nicking flowers," I shouted as I let him in.

The three of us spent the next hour and a half before dinner drinking my dad's homebrew and recording the new records onto cassette tape with my dad's music centre. My dad had always brewed his own beer, it was nasty, and it gave you a banging hangover. Along with many men from his generation, he preferred warm, flat, bitter beer to cold sparkling lager. Still, after the first mouthful, it didn't taste too bad, and it was free. Sim had brought some cool tracks for us to record, including a load of new 'Studio One' stuff. Records were costly in the 70s, and it was almost impossible to find ska, reggae, and rocksteady discs in our local record stores. Sim had Jamaican friends in Leicester, and always got his hands on new imports.

The homebrew started to go down easier as we acclimated to the peculiar taste, and we all got a little bit drunk. After dinner, Sim tried to teach my mam how to dance to ska music, which was a laugh. He tried to teach my dad too, and even though the old man was fond of a good old 'blinky blonky blimey cockney knees up' and could do a fair impersonation of Dick Van Dyke, he wasn't a natural-born 'skanker.'

Sim was good company, and he always brought a party atmosphere with him. He had a thousand stories about life on the fairground. He'd wandered, lost, scared, and hungry, into the Parkers' lives one chilly night three years ago, and he hadn't looked back since. I don't know how much longer he was going to be a gaff lad, but he loved the job.

Some of the fairground workers we knew were in their thirties and forties, and there were some real characters. There was a dwarf from Somerset, predictably called Lofty. He was married to a colossal Amazon of a woman, who was six feet tall and weighed in at twenty-five stones. We often speculated how they managed to do 'it'. Sim reckoned Lofty used a set of grappling hooks to scale his great, pink Rubenesque wife. Tom and I harboured the theory that he probably launched himself off a wardrobe. Either way, they were blissfully happy and had three children—all of them taller than their dad.

Lofty was a real grafter and incredibly strong; he could carry enormous weights despite his size. He was always clowning around, and the kids loved him. He took the inevitable small person jokes with good humour and gave as good as he got. The rough and tumble lifestyle of the fairground worker was no place for oversensitive souls. Tom and I liked him. He didn't let anything get in the way of life.

Joe Parker and his wife Mary Ann had a knack for employing larger than life characters on their fairgrounds. They knew the value of a good Gaff lad, who could work hard with assembly and maintenance and keep the customers happy when the show started. Unlike some travelling showmen, the Parkers paid decent money to their lads and provided them with good bunks and a place to cook their food. Fairground lads generally came from working-class backgrounds and often had slightly roguish pasts. The Parkers expected honesty from their staff though and took a dim view of workers who short-changed their customers.

Regarding backgrounds, though, there were exceptions to the rule, like Byron, a well-spoken young man in his mid-twenties. He'd turned up one evening at the spring fair on Ealing Common three years ago, and according to Sim, he'd offered to work without pay. He told the Parkers he was writing a novel and looking for inspiration. He helped the gaff lads to sheet down that night and the following nights also, and when the fair was pulling down a week later, Byron was there all night, working as hard as any of the other lads.

When the Gaff moved north to the Midlands, Byron followed the convoy of wagons and trailers up the A5, driving a new Mercedes and towing a large smart caravan. He pitched the beautiful, shiny airstream trailer amongst the showman's living wagons at the next venue. He worked the whole summer and refused payment. His once pale skin became brown, his muscles became toned from hard work, and his office-soft hands became calloused. He grew his sensibly short hair into long black corkscrew curls like Marc Bolan's, and he took to wearing a red neckerchief and silk backed waistcoats, which gave him a swashbuckling air.

Before the end of the summer, he was working the big rides with Sim. Byron loved the Waltzer the best, and the customers loved him, especially the girls. He'd charm them with beautiful words and his 'David Essex' gypsy looks. But there were no crass knee tremblers behind the generators for Byron's conquests. His girlfriends were wined and dined in his plush palace on wheels.

He occasionally got blind drunk, recited beautiful self-composed poetry, and sang opera arias in a fine baritone voice to anybody who'd listen to him. If any of the gaff lads ever needed legal advice, help with official forms, or had literacy problems, he gladly and patiently helped them. He was handy when it came to dealing with red-tape, local council bureaucracy, and day to day running of the show. He soon became an integral member of Parker's operation, and was eventually put on the payroll, even though he insisted he didn't need the money. Nobody seemed to know anything about his past. However, there was a rumour he'd been a promising London barrister who'd fallen from grace.

When the fair travelled to Ealing for its single annual London date in the spring, Byron always took the week off. "There may be people there I don't want to see," he'd say mysteriously, and nobody argued with him.

I once asked him if he liked The Ramones. "Not really my kind of thing, Danny, old chap. I much prefer Mozart, though I simply adore Toots and The Maytals, and T.Rex" he replied politely before offering me a *Gauloises,* which nearly made me cough my lungs up.

Fairgrounds were a bit like the foreign legion. They attracted all kinds of people for all sorts of reasons. I hoped Sim would find something great to do with his life before he got much older. At the time, though, being a gaff lad suited him fine. He was good looking, young, funny, and a natural showman. He hopped on and off the Waltzer and the Speedway with maniacal skill, grace, and daring. Sim and Byron were good friends. Byron always said Sim had the 'heart of a poet.'

They both over-wintered in Parker's yard in Bradford, though Byron sometimes disappeared abroad for a few weeks out of season. Showmen always have 'yards' where they can store and fix their machinery to make it ready for the next season—painting, maintenance, electrics, and heavy engineering jobs. Bearings, gears and drive belts often needed replacing on the big rides. The jobs were endless. Sim had a small, old-fashioned touring caravan with a stove in the corner, and he was proud of it. He had a battered old mono record player and his priceless pile of 45s, all reggae, ska, and rock-steady dating from the 1960s to the present time.' Johnny Too Bad' by The Slickers was Sim's all-time favourite song.

At Christmastime, Mam and Sue had sent a parcel to the Bradford yard for Sim, along with a card from us all. I know this little gesture had meant the world to Him. We all knew his story, and we all knew he deserved some kindness. Mary Ann Parker looked after him and doted on him as well. Sim had a close relationship with the Parkers. Years later the Leicestershire children's homes scandal became public knowledge and we all realised how lucky Sim had been to escape.

The fair had two more nights in our village park—the following Friday and Saturday—and they were usually the busiest nights.

"You helping us 'pull-down' this year, lads?" Sim asked.

On the last night of the fair, at eleven PM sharp, the lights went out, the people drifted off home, and the massive job began. Tom and I had helped the Parkers pull-down for a few years. It was hard work for little money, but the atmosphere was terrific, and we enjoyed it.

The White Lion at the Crossroads would stay open late for the showmen and gaff lads, as long as they were quiet and entered through the back door. Parks would stand everybody a pint, and then it was all hands on deck, working by the light of spotlights running off a generator.

The first job was unscrewing hundreds of coloured light bulbs from the rides and stashing them in big wicker baskets. Then we'd take down the beautifully painted rounding boards, wrap them in dustsheets and pack them carefully away. Tom and I usually helped to pull down the Waltzer or the Speedway, because they were the rides that required the most labour. They were more or less the same ride, except the Waltzer had spinning cars instead of fixed wooden animals and motorbikes. The platforms, cars, gratings, tilts, and frames—every last nut and bolt had to be dismantled and loaded onto trucks and trailers. It was a big job and lasted most of the night. By first light, most of the heavy work was usually done, and Mary Ann and her niece, Little Alice, would cook a mountain of bacon and eggs and brew gallons of tea for the workers in the catering trailer.

"Yeah, we'll be there, mate," said Tom and me to Sim. "Wouldn't miss it for the world."

I always thought the field was a sorry looking place after the fair had pulled out. Pale green patches were left where the rides had been, and circular ghost tracks were worn into the grass where the stallholders had plied their orbital trade for a week. The park looked like the front room at home after the Christmas decorations were taken down, a bit boring and workaday. The fair did herald the start of summer for us, though, so we never stayed downhearted for long. Sim's season was only just beginning. He had a whole summer and most of the autumn to look forward to on the road. Hard work and an itinerant lifestyle were the downsides; endless Waltzer acrobatics, new girls in every town, and the feeling of belonging to a family were his consolations.

Later, the three of us—along with Bullshit Dave, rode out to a pub in the neighbouring village to watch a band. We finished the night at Tom's house, where Sue kindly donated a Watneys Party seven to the cause. The Greens had a better telly than ours, and *The Old Grey Whistle Test* was on.

We watched Doctor Feelgood. It was a repeat, but we didn't care because we loved The Feelgoods. The guitarist, Wilko Johnson was zig zagging backwards and forwards across the stage like an automaton. The band were 'full on'. Lee Brillaux was sweating and gurning as he sucked on his tin sandwich and growled out the pub rock classics. Sim wasn't crazy about Rhythm and Blues, but he was happy, flirting outrageously, and dancing with Kim, Trudy, and even Sue. Sim didn't have an 'off' switch.

We watched him, "He just can't bloody help himself, can he?" said Tom, laughing.

Everybody loved Sim.

SEVEN

I Get My Kicks Out On The Floor

PHIL AND SUE had hired the cricket pavilion for Trudy's sixteenth birthday party. They'd booked a mobile disco. My mam and a few more of their friends had made a mountain of food for the party. Trudy had invited loads of her friends from school, a mixture of fifteen- and sixteen-year-old girls and boys from her year. In the pavilion kitchen, there was the usual wine, 'Cherry B' and 'Babycham' for the ladies, and bottles of beer and party sevens for the men. The partygoers were limited to soft drinks, but I think most of them snuck some booze into the party or nicked it from the kitchen. The place was full to bursting with raucous, excited teenagers.

The old wooden windows were running with condensation from the body heat and rattling in their frames to the sound of "Teenage Depression" by Eddie And The Hotrods, which was blasting out of the PA system. The DJ was excellent. He seemed to have the measure of the audience, and he spun all the right records from the old classics to new punk tracks.

I walked into the room and spotted Trudy. Predictably, she'd had a ton of new clothes for her birthday. She was dressed to kill, and she looked lovely. She and Kim had their usual entourage of lovesick fourth year boys hanging around them, and they'd both managed to get a little bit drunk by the time I turned up. Trudy had a bottle of sherry hidden in her bag, and she and Kim were slipping outside frequently and swigging it like a couple of winos. For her birthday, I'd blown a big chunk of my wages on a little silver letter "T" on a chain, and she was wearing it.

The room was dark. Layers of cigarette smoke reflected the disco lights over the dance floor, while the ubiquitous disco mirror ball dotted the dancers with lights. The unmistakable intro of the old Doby Gray track "Out On the Floor" came blasting through the PA bins, and the small, creaking dance floor was packed instantly.

Northern soul music had always been popular in the village. Some of us older kids had made the pilgrimage to the northern clubs, and it had been mind-blowing.

The Wigan Casino had opened in 1973, and Tom and I had been amongst the first kids from our village to go there. We'd bussed it up there on my fourteenth birthday and queued for five hours on the door. A bloke had sold us some blue pills for two bob each, but they didn't have any effect on us. They were probably aspirin dipped in food colouring. That was mine and Tom's only experience with drugs during our teenage years, apart from smoking a bit of dope.

The atmosphere at the Casino was electric, and the dancing was inspiring. It was beautiful. Kids had turned up from all over the country. Everybody was just there for the music. No fights, no trouble, just a shared love of northern soul and dancing. We hitchhiked home the next day and got into a load of trouble with our parents. We were both grounded for two weeks, but it was worth it. We'd been back a couple of times since, and every time, it just got better.

Despite my terrible sense of rhythm, I actually wasn't too bad at northern soul dancing.

I spotted Tom; he was already on the dance floor. He was an excellent northern soul dancer. He'd mastered all the classic moves, spins, and fancy footwork. People were giving him plenty of space rather than risk a kung fu kick in the head. Even the younger kids danced to this track. Everybody loved it, along with Tami Lynn's "I'm Gonna Run Away From You" and R Dean Taylor's "There's a Ghost in My House." It was a guaranteed floor-filler.

The DJ slowed it down with the next record: "Let's Get it On" by Marvin Gaye. Trudy made a beeline for me. She threw her arms around my neck and we started dancing.

"Do I get a birthday kiss, Fonzie?"

"Yeah, of course," I said.

I went to give her an innocent little kiss, but she grabbed me around the neck in an iron grip and started giving me a full-on sherry-infused snog. It was like being kissed by a small, passionate trifle. She danced close and ground herself hard against me. I was glad the lights were low because I was probably going to have a slight trouser predicament after this dance.

I needn't have worried, though. An antidote was close at hand.

I glanced over Trudy's shoulder at the kitchen, where the adults were standing, drinking, chatting, and watching the dance floor. I caught sight of Phil looking at us, unsmiling, with a raised eyebrow. It's what Tom and I called his dad's death stare. It was also an effective method of birth control. I can't say that I wasn't enjoying kissing his daughter, but the look he was giving me had the same effect as having my testicles crushed in a vice. I wrestled myself free from Trudy with some lame excuse about needing some fresh air and escaped outside until things had cooled down a bit.

Later, with half a dozen Brandy and Babychams inside her, Sue hit the dance floor. She looked stunning, wearing tight jeans and a white, 'lace up' top. She was dancing with a group of girls, including Kim and Trudy, to "Black is Black," the Belle Epoque disco song. Most of the teenage boys in the room were watching her every move and probably committing the image to memory for later use.

I would have loved to have asked Sue for a slow dance, but I didn't want to risk another one of her husband's testicle-withering stares.

The night was a load of fun, and the birthday girl had a great time. She drank way too much sherry, and later on, she threw up spectacularly on a poor boy who had been trying to pluck up the courage to ask her out. She'd kissed her older brother's best friend, passionately, in front of her school friends, and she'd pissed her dad off into the bargain. In Trudy's estimation, that was a good night's work.

———

Phil called me into the site hut on Monday morning. It was a big, old mobile home that was towed onto whichever site we were working on. Sue and Phil used one end as an office, and we used the other end for brewing our tea and playing cards when we got rained off. Sue didn't get into work until ten AM most days, so it was just the two of us for a friendly, cosy little chat. I wasn't surprised. I'd been expecting it.

Phil cleared his throat and began his speech.

"Daniel, look, mate… I just wanted a little word with you about our Trudy. You know Sue and I think the world of you, lad. Trudy does too, though I suppose you know that already. I also know that you and Tom always look out for her, even though she can be a right pain in the arse sometimes, and we're grateful for that. I just want to ask you to remember that she's only just turned sixteen, Dan. Do you know what I mean?"

Phil was finding the conversation a little awkward. I was too. I could have protested and told him that Trudy had virtually overpowered me on the dancefloor on Saturday night, but that sounded like a ridiculous excuse, and I didn't exactly fight her off. So, I told Phil that I understood exactly what he meant and that he needn't worry.

"Thanks, Danny," he said. I think he was relieved that we understood each other.

Trudy was the apple of his eye, and I guess he thought that her sixteenth birthday was like the first day of open season for the young bloods of the village. The last thing he wanted was his cute little daughter coming home with a cute little bump in her belly. Recently, she'd changed from a pretty little kid into a stunning young woman, and I didn't even see it happen. I just looked at her one day and thought to myself, *Wow! Where did little Trudy go?*

I didn't expect that she was serious about me, though. I thought I was probably just a handy prop to impress her school friends.

Tom and I had been spending quite a lot of time with Trudy and Kim recently. We'd see them in the youth club or at the disco or sometimes take them with us to the Rendezvous or up to Jack's Hill Cafe on the back of our bikes. The four of us always had a laugh together, even though Trudy could sometimes wind her brother up like a clock.

After Phil's little chat, though, I thought it was probably time to cool things down a bit, especially with the prospect of spending two weeks with the girls on holiday. Besides, Tom and I had decided that we were going to concentrate mainly on chasing girls in Spain. We were going to be legends on the Costa Brava, leaving a trail of broken hearts behind us. They'd be talking about us for years to come in the bars and discos—the two bronzed English demigods in Ramones T-shirts who'd deflowered a resort full of teenage girls, then left them heartbroken.

Well, that was the plan anyway.

EIGHT

Yes, Sir, I Can Boogie

THE FOUR OF us squeezed into the big, plush leather back seat of Phil's Rover P6. It was a top of the range motor with a 3.5-litre engine, a bit different to my dad's Vauxhall Viva. Sue had warned us all not to bring too much luggage because there wouldn't be much room for it in the boot of the car.

"You'll only need T-shirts, shorts, bathers, and something smart to wear on the flight and in the evenings," she'd said. Then she'd proceeded to pack a massive case full of clothes for herself.

Trudy and Kim also had large suitcases. "Girls need more things than boys," Trudy had said, smiling sweetly at me when I'd remarked on the size of their cases.

We were flying from Luton. Trudy and Kim kept us amused for most of the drive down the M1 with their Lorraine Chase impersonations. "Were you truly wafted here from paradise? Nah, Luton airport."

When they'd done that one to death, they went on to treat us all to a choice of popular music of the day.

They sang tunelessly along to the radio. They were pretty, but they couldn't sing. Nobody cared, though. We were in the holiday mood, excited, laughing, and joking.

Once we'd checked in, Phil and Sue made straight for the terminal bar. Tom and I followed them, and the girls headed for the shops. Sue claimed she was a nervous flyer and needed some 'Dutch courage,' but Phil said, "It's just an excuse to get some brandy and Baby-cham down your neck."

He got the drinks in, and we sat down. "Cheers, happy holidays," said Phil, raising his pint glass.

I loved being with these people. They were my other family.

Half an hour later, the girls came back smelling of a heady mix of multiple perfumes and wearing liberal applications of vivid makeup.

It was the first time Kim and I had flown, so we were excited. Sue had insisted that everybody dressed up for the flight, so Tom and I were looking uncommonly smart for once. We wore two-tone tonic suits, Ben Sherman shirts, and loafers. There was a party atmosphere on the plane. Everybody was excited and enjoying themselves. We taxied onto the runway, and the pilot slowly built up the revs in the big jet engines until they were screaming. Then he let the brakes off with a bang, and we were slammed back into our seats as the plane leapt forward. It was better than any rollercoaster rides I'd ever been on.

I was amazed how quickly we climbed up through the grey and into the beautiful blue sky above. I'd never realised that there was always a sunny day trapped on the other side of the clouds.

The smiling stewardesses were pretty and glamorous. They served drinks, so we all had one, and later, they served us meals on partitioned metal trays like the ones they use in prisons. Smoking was only allowed at the rear of the plane, and every ten minutes, one of us nipped off for a cigarette. Kim didn't smoke, and Trudy only pretended she did. She often used a cigarette as a prop when she wanted to look more grown-up.

The whole cabin started to fill up with smoke as the flight progressed. Trudy remarked that having a smoking section on an airplane was like "having a peeing area in a public swimming pool."

Kim followed up with, "Or a farting area on a bus. 'Kindly take your bottom problem to the trumping area at the rear of the coach, Miss Green,'" she said in her best Mrs Slocombe accent. As usual, the two of them laughed hysterically at their own jokes.

Getting into the mood, Phil added, "Or a shouting area in a library."

But the girls just looked at him without smiling. Trudy said, "Yeah, but that's not funny, though, Dad," and that made them laugh even more.

Trudy and Kim inhabited a surreal teenage world of their own. Tom and I usually understood them, but most adults weren't on the same wavelength. Sue Green was the exception, though. She could usually be just as daft as them.

The aircraft began its descent into Girona airport, and soon we touched down on the sunbaked runway to a round of applause from the passengers. The cabin doors opened, and we stepped out onto the stairway, blasted by the full force of a midday Spanish sun. I'd never felt anything quite like it. The air, even though it was mixed with the kerosene fumes from the jet engines, smelled hot, spicy, and foreign. And the sky was a perfect, flawless azure, marred only by the criss-cross vapour trails of the passenger jets.

After we'd collected our luggage, and found our holiday rep. We were herded onto a bus along with thirty or so other British tourists. The bus headed down the *autopista* and then across the country a few miles to Lloret De Mar.

At Lloret was a broad crescent of golden sand packed with holidaymakers, bordered by an impossibly blue sea. Bikini-clad girls were everywhere I looked. We'd left behind a grey English summer, and landed in teenage heaven. Our hotel was impressive as well, with a huge pool area at the front and an elegant, marbled reception. It was a million miles away from the dingy, cabbage-smelling guest houses that my parents used to take us to when we were kids, in Llandudno, Cromer, or Skegness.

At the front desk, we were given the keys to three adjacent rooms on the fourth floor. Each room had great views of the beach and a large balcony separated by screen block walls, which were low enough to talk to our neighbours over. There was a bar and a concert room with nightly entertainment. According to the poster in reception, that night's treat was an overweight Elvis impersonator in a nylon jumpsuit.

Tom and I stood leaning on the balcony railings and drinking in the view of our playground for the next two weeks. We could already see Kim and Trudy making a beeline for the beach over the road. They were bikinied, suntan oiled, and eliciting attention from the Spanish waiters working the poolside bar at the front of the hotel. I wolf-whistled loudly, and Trudy replied with a V sign and a smile.

Once we'd changed back into our 'all-American punk' T-shirts and jeans, Tom and I hit the baking hot streets. There were girls everywhere. French girls, English girls, German, and Spanish girls. Girls in bikinis. Girls around the pool. Girls on the beach, sunbathing topless!

"This beats the crap outta Cromer, doesn't it, mate?" said Tom.

"It's bloody paradise," I replied as we headed for the street that had all the bars.

Signs advertised Double Diamond beer, fish and chips, English breakfasts, Guinness, Ye Olde Tea Shoppe, Piccadilly pub, and Paddy's bar.

"Bloody hell, Tom," I said, "it's just like Skeggy."

"Yeah, but without the hypothermic blue-legged girls and drizzle," he replied, laughing.

We dove into a busy pavement bar, and Tom slightly smugly ordered, *"Dos cervezas, por favor,"* using nearly the full extent of his Spanish vocabulary in one vital sentence. The waiter came back with two glasses, frosted with ice and containing the sweetest, coldest, most delicious beer I'd ever tasted.

Two girls appeared from the busy street. They were

pretty, wearing bikini tops and shorts. Tom immediately stood up and guided them over to our table. "Two comfy seats over here in the shade. Come and sit down ladies, I'll get you a drink."

Bloody hell, he was good! It was like watching a sheepdog at work.

The girls told us where all the hotspots were in Lloret and which bars and discos were the best. They were from Somerset and spoke with lazy, west country drawls, which we thought were quite exotic. Unfortunately, they were on holiday with their boyfriends, who were watching football on TV in another bar.

Tom wasn't downbeat, though. When the girls had gone, he said, "It's all good chat up practice, Danny boy, and God knows you need it."

He was right. I'd always been a bit shy when it came to chatting up girls, but I was learning from the master. That night, we hit the town. The west country girls had recommended a nightspot called Flamingos.

"You'll love it there," they'd told us, smiling prettily through their clotted cream accents. So, after dinner at the hotel and a few drinks around the bars, Tom and I headed off to find the place.

It was a big, smart, impressive venue with flashing lights shining out onto the street, and the sound of disco music pumped out into the warm evening. We walked into a trendy, plush nightclub with a large, spot lit dance floor. It took our eyes a little while to adjust to the dark interior as we made our way to the bar to get a drink. The new Donna Summer track, "I Feel Love," was blasting out of the sound system, and the dance floor was busy.

"Fancy a dance?" asked Tom.

"Nah, you know I can't dance to this disco shit. I'll ask the DJ if he's got any ska or punk rock," I replied.

The British DJ looked at me a bit strangely when I asked. "No, sorry. We don't get much call for that kind of music here," he replied with a Larry Grayson pout that should've set the alarm bells ringing.

I walked back to the bar and told Tom the bad news. He just shrugged and said, "Well, I'm gonna have a dance anyway."

The next track the DJ played was "Yes Sir I Can Boogie" by the Spanish duo Baccara. We'd only heard it a couple of times back home, but here in Lloret, it was being constantly played in every bar on the strip. Kim and Trudy had been belting it out in painful wails as well.

"Shame there's not many girls. The place probably gets busy later. I wouldn't even be surprised if those two birds from Somerset don't give their boyfriends the slip and come and join us," shouted Tom above the music as he made his way onto the dance floor.

Tom loved to dance. He was a natural. Pretty soon, people were giving him some space and watching his moves. Before too long, a couple of guys were dancing next to him. Then a boy started dancing opposite him. Soon Tom was at the centre of a circle of enthusiastically gyrating, trendy young men with porn star moustaches. That was when I realised that the girls had sent us to Lloret's only gay disco. Tom, who'd been oblivious to everything except his fancy footwork, twigged the situation at about the same time I did.

He stopped dancing and walked back to the bar to find me doubled up with laughter.

"Those bloody little mares," he said, laughing. "They must be sitting in a bar somewhere, pissing themselves."

"Oh, Tom," I said, wringing my hands, "look at the hearts you've broken tonight."

We drank up and left the club. It was a nice place with a good atmosphere, but we weren't going to find any girls there. I minced a little on the way out and tried to hold Tom's hand, but he punched me hard on the arm. I couldn't wait to tell Trudy and Kim.

Back at the hotel, we caught the last half of the Elvis extravaganza. The concert room was packed to the rafters with partying holidaymakers, mostly Brits but some French and Germans as well. Everybody was having a great time, drinking, dancing, and singing along to the music.

The Spanish Elvis and his band were actually quite entertaining. *Señor* Presley had covered the rock 'n' roll years in his first set.

Sue said it was terrific. "You should've seen him in his gold lamé jacket doing 'Jailhouse Rock.' The old man and I were up and jiving."

She told us Trudy and Kim had got a bit fed up with the Elvis show, and were off somewhere doing their own thing. They turned up later, halfway through "The Las Vegas Years" and found Tom and me propping up the bar, eyeing up the girls on the dance floor.

I told them about the Flamingos fiasco, and they laughed so loudly that they almost drowned out "Suspicious Minds."

Later, as the rotund rocker crooned "The Wonder Of You" in a Spanish accent, Tom danced with Kim, and I danced with Sue. Slightly tipsy, Trudy accused me of being a pervert. "Dancing with a woman who's old enough to be your mother is just disgusting," she said, but I think she was only joking.

We all got wonderfully drunk on the cold beer and monster-sized shots of brandy, rum 'n' black, and vodka and orange. We laughed until our faces ached. Our first night in Lloret had been fantastic. I loved Spain, but it was going to get even better.

NINE

Groovy Situation

WE FIRST SAW her when Tom and I were sitting outside of a bar called The OK Corral.

It was one of those tacky, touristy bars with Watney's Red Barrel and Guinness on tap, as well as the cold Spanish beer that we liked so much. We could order any kind of food we desired here as long as it was deep-fried and in a greasy, plastic basket. It was right up our street and we loved it.

She was sitting a few tables away on her own, without a drink. Petite and suntanned, she was wearing denim shorts with one slim brown leg crossed over the other. Her arms were also brown and slender, and she wore several silver bangles on her wrists. Her long chestnut hair tumbled over her shoulders.

She took off the sunglasses she was wearing, linked her hands, stretched her arms above her head, and glanced our way. She smiled at us. Her smile was wonderful, like sunshine. It was like being noticed by a divine being. She had warm hazel eyes and perfect white teeth. I'd never seen anybody quite so utterly gorgeous in my life, and I felt immediately embarrassed that she'd caught me watching her so intently.

Tom had seen her as well. "Cor blimey, Dan! She's gorgeous," he said under his breath.

Just then, a young man with a long mullet hairstyle walked out of the bar, placed two coffee cups on the table, and sat down opposite her.

My heart sank. "Oh, crap! She's got a boyfriend. They always do, don't they?"

"Yeah, hard luck, mate. Looks like 'Hairdo' got there first," said Tom.

My existence had just been acknowledged by the singularly most beautiful and exotic creature I'd ever seen in my life, and then in the next instant, my dreams had been shattered. I couldn't even treat myself to a brief flight of fantasy. She was somebody else's dream girl. Even worse, he had a long, black mullet like Alvin Stardust. How did boys with such uncool hairstyles get girls like that? We'd gotten rid of our mullets in 1974. Life was so unfair!

A year ago, I'd had a massive crush on the girl who worked behind the counter in our local chemist store. She was a pretty blonde with big green eyes and cupid's bow lips. She wore the usual chemist shop garb: a white lab coat and Scholl sandals, which was probably the most unsexy combination of workwear ever contrived, but even so, I thought she was gorgeous. I went into the shop so many times just to catch a glimpse of her that I had the biggest collection of plastic combs and toothbrushes in the midlands. This infatuation lasted for about a month.

Then I bumped into a girl coming out of the corner shop and accidentally knocked her ice cream out of her hand. She was wearing a tight T-shirt with a plunging neckline, and she had the most incredible breasts I'd ever seen in my life. At least half of the jettisoned ninety-nine cornet was lodged in her fantastic, cleavage. I had a strong but momentary compulsion to bury my head in her breasts and pluck the chocolate flake out with my teeth. Instead, I gave her my hankie and stutteringly apologised like a village idiot.

She smiled sweetly as she popped the flake into her mouth and mopped the melting ice cream from her heavenly torso. She told me it didn't matter because she was trying to lose some weight anyway. And so, another case of unrequited love was born.

To this day, I can't look at a Cadbury's flake without thinking of Rubenesque girls in tight T-shirts. I think I spent most of the hot summer of 76 with a boner.

At the time, I'd put those fleeting infatuations down to my fickle nature and fascination with female anatomy, but the girl sitting at the table a few yards away was different. My stomach was full of butterflies, and I felt slightly light-headed. A primaeval switch had been flicked in my brain. I wanted that girl with a passion I'd never known before.

Even Tom noticed. "You okay, mate?" he asked, looking amused. "You look a bit strange. I mean, even stranger than you usually do."

"It's just that girl, Tom," I stammered stupidly. "She's just so bloody beautiful."

Then incredibly, she turned her head and looked right at me, almost as if she could hear what I was saying. She smiled that smile again, and I smiled back. Then we held each other's eyes for a fraction more time than was normal.

The girl and the mullet head talked for a while. I watched them. They didn't seem to act like a couple— more like a brother and sister. I started to feel a tiny bit optimistic. When they'd finished their drinks, they stood up to leave. Most of the guys in the bar had noticed her also and were watching her walk away.

She was just so wonderfully cute. She looked back at me once more before they turned the corner at the end of the street.

"I reckon she's a bit of a flirt," said Tom. "I mean, she's out for a drink with her boyfriend, and she was deffo giving you the eye. Brazen hussy if you ask me, mate."

"Maybe Hairdo's not her boyfriend," I said.

Tom just laughed. "Don't get your hopes up, Danny. Anyway, look around you. There are pretty girls everywhere. You don't need to fall for the only one you can't have."

Tom was right. We'd met some girls from Manchester on the beach earlier and arranged to meet them in a bar that night. They were nice and a lot of fun, and we were looking forward to seeing them. But the girl with the chestnut hair was just something else.

I spent the rest of the day thinking about her. I

looked out for her on the beach and in the bars, but it seemed she'd disappeared.

The next afternoon, Tom and I went back to the OK Corral. I was still holding on to the faint hope of seeing the girl again, and miraculously, there she was. She was sitting at the same table, only this time, she was with a girl about the same age as herself. My heart jumped in my chest. She was even more gorgeous than I'd remembered.

She saw me and smiled at me. I nearly glanced behind me just to check that she wasn't smiling at someone else. Then, almost in a daze, feeling uncommonly brave and to Tom's utter amazement, I walked right up to the table and asked if they minded if we sat with them.

"*Si, claro*. That would be nice," she said, smiling that incredibly disarming smile again.

We sat down and ordered some drinks for us all. The girl told me her name was Elena, and her friend was Isabel. Tom and I introduced ourselves quite formally, holding out our hands, only to feel a bit daft when the girls leant over the table to kiss us on each cheek in the Spanish way.

They spoke English well, quite slowly and with strong Spanish accents. Elena told me she was seventeen years old; her birthday had been the week before. She'd come to Lloret for a month and was attending one of the many language schools around the resort. Her parents had a campsite at a place called Albarracin in north-eastern Spain. This was the second summer she'd been to the language school and her second week in Lloret. Even with my poor math skills, I quickly figured out that if I were lucky, I could possibly spend at least a week and a half in the company of this goddess.

She'd learned English at her regular school back home, but her parents were keen that she improved. The tourist industry was taking off in northern Spain, and she told me that Albarracin was a beautiful and ancient place which was visited by people from all over the world. Elena's aunt and uncle lived in Lloret De Mar, so, conveniently, she stayed with them in their apartment.

Isabel was her friend from the language school. She was sixteen, a little taller than Elena, good looking, with long, jet-black hair and smiling brown eyes. Her dad owned the local cinema, and she'd lived in Lloret all her life. The girls had lessons in the mornings, starting early, but the afternoons and evenings were their own.

I could have listened to Elena talk forever. She was animated and captivating, and she looked straight into my eyes when she spoke. It turned out that the mullet haired fellow was her older, married cousin, Pedro. If he'd been there, I would have kissed him with joy.

Tom seemed to be getting on well with Isabel. She was laughing out loud at something he'd said. Tom found it easy to chat to girls, and girls liked him. My mam always said Tom could charm the birds out of the trees.

We sat and talked for more than an hour. Elena wanted to know all about my life in England and my family, and she told me all about herself. She'd lived in her hometown all her life, and her dad had opened the campsite ten years earlier. The business was good, and the whole family worked there, including herself, her older married sister, her younger brother, and her mam and dad.

I told her about our village, my job, my family, I told her about the village disco, the funfair, our friend Sim. I even mentioned Bullshit Dave. I think I was just babbling on about anything to try and keep her attention. Amazingly, though, she seemed to be hanging on my every word.

We talked about music. She liked the Ramones, which she pronounced the *Ram-on-ez*. She'd never heard of The Stranglers, Doctor Feelgood, or Toots and The Maytals, though, so I told her I'd give her a cassette. She even seemed to be interested in motorbikes, but she might have been humouring me because she didn't seem to understand even the most basic principles of two-stroke tuning. I didn't care, though. I just wanted to talk to her and see her smile. I just wanted to hear her voice and look into those beautiful eyes.

At around five PM, she'd promised to collect her younger cousin, Marta, from the beach and walk her home to Pedro's house, so we all arranged to meet later that evening. The girls walked off together, arm in arm.

Tom, laughing, clapped me on the back. "Who's a dark horse, then, Danny?"

Both pretty pleased with ourselves, we went back to the hotel for dinner, even though I was so excited that I couldn't eat a thing. Trudy and Kim asked us if we were going to the hotel disco that night, and Tom told them we had something else on.

"What, more dancing with the boys at Flamingos tonight, is it, Tom?" said Kim, winking at him.

Trudy and Kim were getting some mileage out of the gay disco story, and I kind of regretted telling them. Even Phil was getting in on the act. "Off out tonight, lads? Don't forget your handbags, or you won't have anything to dance around."

This story would be around the building site like wildfire when we got home.

By seven o'clock that evening, we were waiting for the Spanish girls back at the OK Corral. We watched them walk up the street, arm in arm. They looked stunning. Elena was wearing a yellow dress that came to just above her knees. The colour suited her perfectly. They waved when they saw us, and I noticed a few envious looks from the other boys in the bar. I felt incredibly proud when she sat down, facing me, and smiled. I felt like her smile was just for me. We all sat and talked for a while and then walked along the seafront together.

The high summer evening sun was still beating down, and the beach was still busy. We stopped at a tapas bar that the girls knew. Isabel's father and Elena's uncle were regulars. The bar was used mainly by Spanish locals. Tourists were welcome, but there were no jugs of sangria and no disco music playing, only local radio stations playing Spanish songs. The air con was still running flat out in the bar, and it was good to get out of the heat. Some old boys were playing dominos, slamming the pieces down hard on the tabletops, cursing and laughing. Other young people were in the bar as well, eating food and drinking cold beer and *tinto de verano*.

The girls ordered some tapas for us all with the drinks. The food had a bit more garlic than I was used to, but it was delicious. Sitting opposite me, Elena's hands were on the tabletop, and I really wanted to hold them, but I just couldn't pluck up the courage. It was like a wonderful dream. Everything was golden—the sun, the beach—and there were little flecks of gold in her hazel eyes.

Elena asked me if I had a girlfriend in England. I told her I didn't. I asked her if she had a boyfriend, and thankfully, she said no. I found that a bit hard to believe, so I asked her if the boys in Albarracin were blind or stupid. She blushed a little bit, smiled at me, and said she hadn't met the right boy in Albarracin.

We told the girls about our trip to Flamingos, and they laughed a lot. Flamingos was well known to the locals in the town, and they couldn't believe that we hadn't noticed we were in a gay bar. I had to repeat the bit about Tom being surrounded by trendy young men on the dancefloor three times and only stopped when the mascara was running down their cheeks.

We left the bar after a while and carried on walking along the seafront, heading towards the quieter end of the beach. Elena and I were walking twenty yards or so behind Tom and Isabel. We were talking a lot, getting used to each other's accents. Feeling suddenly very brave, I reached out for her hand. It felt small and delicate in mine. She looked at me and smiled shyly. It was the first time we'd touched, and it felt like electricity.

My heart was beating like crazy. I think she liked me too.

At the hotel earlier that afternoon, I'd frantically tried to learn some Spanish from my dog-eared phrase-book to try and impress her. She was kind about my terrible pronunciation, and now she tried to teach me how to pronounce Albarracin. She rolled her Rs like a snare drum solo, but I could never do that.

We stopped walking, and she faced me. "Look at what I do with my tongue, then you try."

I watched her mouth closely, trying to figure out how she did it. I tried, but I found it impossible and just made strange, imbecilic noises every time I attempted it. She laughed out loud at my efforts. Feeling a bit foolish, I told her it didn't matter because R rolling wasn't some-thing the English concerned themselves with anyway, and she laughed even more.

I loved to hear her laugh. She had a loud and surprisingly raucous laugh for such a small and pretty girl. To me, though, it was the most beautiful sound in the world.

She tried one more time. She faced me again and told me to watch her mouth carefully while she pronounced the word. I did, and then, suddenly, we were kissing, and she smelled faintly of garlic. The noise from the seafront bars and restaurants seemed to disappear. It was like we were the only two people in the world that existed.

And that's how a working-class boy from England who'd spent his whole life so far treating the smell of garlic with mild suspicion decided that it was actually the most beautiful scent in the world.

We walked on without saying much, though we were holding hands quite tightly.

Something profound had happened. I didn't know it at the time, but the wheels of destiny had started to turn. This wasn't like the girl in the chemist shop, the ice cream girl, or any other girl I'd ever known. This time, I think I'd fallen in love.

"C'mon, you two, keep up!" shouted Tom from fifty yards in front. "We're ready for a beer."

He and Isabel were arm in arm and heading for a bar on the other side of the road. There was a Guinness sign over the door and a chalkboard bearing the message 'Sunday roasts with Bisto gravy.'

"Ain't Gonna Bump No More (With No Big Fat Woman)" was blasting out of the speakers under the shady awning. It looked like we'd discovered another little cultural gem for homesick Brits. We sat at a table and admired the tasteful array of plastic crabs and lobsters hanging from the old fishing net on the bar's outside wall. Elena tried to order the drinks in Spanish, but the English waiter couldn't understand her, so she had to order them in English.

We spent the rest of the evening lying on the warm rocks at the far end of the beach as the sun went down. I walked Elena back to her aunt's apartment around midnight, and we kissed goodnight on the doorstep. Walking back to the hotel, I felt like I was floating on air and I could move mountains. All of those stupid clichés that people allude to about being in love, I realised they were actually true.

TEN

Spanish Stroll

Tom and I lay on our beds talking into the early hours. We could hear Trudy and Kim in the room next door, music playing full blast, laughing out loud. They were like teenage vampires on holiday; they never seemed to sleep.

We'd been spending every possible minute with the Spanish girls, so we hadn't seen much of Trudy and Kim for the last few days. It seemed they'd got a whole new entourage though. Poor old Phil was having a hell of a job, vetting boys, and keeping amorous Spanish waiters and barmen away from the two girls (and his wife).

Trudy and Kim had been spending time with some English boys they'd met, who were the same age as them. I think Tom was a little bit jealous on account of having a 'thing' for Kim, but he knew the age difference between them was taboo according to our unwritten teenage protocol.

If a sixteen-going-on-seventeen-year-old boy dated a

fifteen-year-old girl, he'd be labelled a 'cradle snatcher' by his mates, forever.

Right now, Tom had Isabel on his mind. "I like her a lot, Dan, but I don't want to get too fond of her because it won't be long until we're saying goodbye. She's cute, though, and a lot of fun. What about Elena, though? Bloody hell, mate, when's the wedding?"

I laughed. "Don't worry, Tom. You're gonna be the best man."

The girls were singing next door. I think they were experimenting with harmonies. It was bloody horrible.

Tom banged on the wafer-thin wall. "Oi! Keep the noise down, you pair of tarts!"

"Get stretched, knobhead!" came the succinct and predictable reply.

We went out onto the balcony for a smoke. It was a tiny bit cooler outside but still hot. I loved leaning on the balcony railings, seeing the lights strung along the seafront, and hearing the gentle surf breaking on the beach across the street. I wished we could stay there forever in the hotel, and I could see the Spanish girl every day. The thought of saying goodbye to her was hanging over my head like a black cloud. I tried not to think about it, but it kept creeping back into my mind, and when it did, my stomach lurched like crazy.

Trudy and Kim had guessed that Tom and I had been seeing some girls, but they hadn't seen us with them yet, despite a couple of attempts to follow us, which we'd foiled by dodging through some back streets.

Sue had been curious as well. "C'mon, you two,

when are we going to meet these mystery girls? Why don't we all go out for dinner one night?"

We'd just laughed it off. We weren't quite sure how Elena and Isabel would take to the full onslaught of cheeky teenage banter that Trudy and Kim would undoubtedly assault them with.

The girls appeared on their balcony next door. "Kim and I are starting a band. That's why we're practicing," said Trudy, obviously a bit tipsy from a night on the town. "Why don't you and Tom start one? You could call yourselves 'The Village Idiots.'"

They both dissolved into laughter.

Leaning over the adjoining wall, Trudy reached out and gave my Hugh Cornwall quiff an annoying ruffle.

"C'mon, then, Fonzie. Give us a fag and tell us all about these old bags you've been meeting. 'Cause we're gonna find out anyway," added Kim.

"I don't think there are any girls, Kim," said Trudy, turning to her friend. "I think these two are just perving around the beaches all day, looking for topless girls to snap with Dan's Instamatic."

"That's actually not a bad idea," Tom replied. "We were looking for something to do in the morning, weren't we, Dan?"

"How're things going with the boys from Derby?" I asked.

"Oh, okay," said Kim, waving her hand graciously. "We give them a couple of hours of our company when we're feeling generous, don't we, Trude?"

"Yeah," replied Trudy. "We are kinda 'in-demand' on the Costa Brava don't you know."

Tom and I laughed. "You'd better go and get your beauty sleep, then, and leave us to plan our perving trip to the beach".

They finally caught up with us the next evening, though. We were sitting outside of a bar at the end of the strip. We didn't know if they were following us, or maybe they just found us by chance, but we hadn't seen them at this end of town before.

With trepidation, I introduced Trudy and Kim to our girlfriends. I told them that the girls were Spanish, and they'd maybe have to speak a little bit slower than usual as they weren't used to our midlands accents.

"Cheeky git," said Trudy. "Whaddya mean, accents? We speak the queen's English in Lestah."

Trudy held out her hand to Elena. I was expecting the worst.

She smiled cheekily and said, "*Ho-lah*, you speaky Eenglish?"

She spoke to my girlfriend as if she were a Martian invader.

Elena smiled, shook her hand, and said, "Yes, of course. You speaky Spanish?"

Magnanimously, Elena offered the girls a Spanish cigarette.

"No, thanks, darling," said Trudy, smiling sweetly. "These foreign ones make me cough. I find them a bit crude, to be honest."

Tom and I were enjoying the exchange immensely. It was like watching a verbal boxing match.

Trudy pulled out a packet of Players Number 6 that she'd probably had in her handbag for the last six months and said, "Try one of these English ones. They're much nicer."

"No thanks, love," said Elena using a term she'd borrowed from Tom and me. She even flattened the vowel and got the midlands accent just right. "I find the English ones a bit short, and they have very little taste."

"Wow, your English is good," countered Trudy. "I bet you can read all the English menus in the restaurants, especially the ones with the pictures."

"Yes, I been taking extra lessons," said Elena, smiling at me and reaching to squeeze my hand.

Trudy knew she'd met her match. "C'mon, Kim. Let's go and find some life in this dump."

As a parting shot directed at Tom and me, Trudy called back, "Surprised to see you two here. To be honest, we thought you'd be out on the town, dancing with the boys."

We all laughed. Trudy was on form.

Elena said, "Your sister, Tom, she's a *duende*."

"A do-what?" asked Tom.

They explained the word to us. *Duende* had a few subtle meanings in Spanish, but in this case, the closest translation was a mischievous spirit.

Tom smiled. "You've got her sussed, girl."

The next few afternoons we spent together. We'd wait outside the school for the girls to finish class and then go to the beach together. We sunbathed on the flat, rocky outcrop at the quieter end of the seafront, swam in the crystal-clear water, and hiring *pedalos* we raced each other in the beautiful millpond flat bay.

In the evenings, we always met at the OK Corral. It was the tackiest bar on the street, but the girls liked it as much as Tom and I. We'd order jugs of *tinto de verano*, glasses of frosted beer, and the cold, dry Spanish sherry that the girls had introduced us to. It was nothing like the sickly cream sherry we had back home, favoured by vicars, winos and great aunts or poured by the bottle full into Christmas trifles by our mams.

Tom and I were even developing a taste for Spanish food. Isabel and Elena dared us to try the snails in the tapas bar. Tom and I never backed down on a dare, but when the snails were placed on the bar top in front of us by a grinning barman, in little terracotta dishes and swimming in a heavy garlic sauce, we looked at each other in horror. Pulling them out of their shells with the small forks provided, we got on with the grim task, but actually, they were pretty good.

"Mmm, rubbery," we remarked, squinting our eyes at each other, paraphrasing the old Benny Hill joke.

We asked the girls why they weren't having any, and Isabel replied, laughing, "We don't like them. They look 'orrible."

The Spanish girls had no school on Saturday, so we went on a train trip to Barcelona. They wanted to show us the sights, and we were looking forward to it.

We took a bus to the neighbouring resort town of Blanes, and from there, we caught the train down the coast to Barcelona. On the train, we laughed and joked and tried to teach each other slang and swear words. "Ooh, ya bugger," in a midlands accent was a good one for the girls. They even managed to make it sound sexy.

Isabel tried to teach us her father's favourite curse. It was about three minutes long and involved shitting on a multitude of saints from a great height and wishing the local mayor a slow and painful death. The girls told us that Spanish curses often start with "*Me cago en todo lo que se menea.*" (That means, "I shit on everything that moves.") The Spanish specialise in long, creative, and colourful curses and often like to involve religion in their elaborate onslaughts. They could never be satisfied with a quick, "Bugger it," or a terse "Oh, fuck." They made British swearers sound like guests at the vicar's tea party.

We taught them some of our local Leicestershire sayings. "Y'all right, me duck?" was a standard greeting back home. They got the accent bang on. It was hilarious hearing pretty Spanish girls talking like Leicester factory women.

The train arrived in the city. We came out of the *Estacion Plaza Catalunya*, blinking into the blazing sunshine, and right into the heart of the most buzzing city in Spain. We walked down the Ramblas, a mile-long, tree-lined walkway. It was high season for tourists, and there were buskers and street traders every few yards.

An old man was selling live snails from a big wicker basket. He had a greasy cigarette hanging out of the corner of his mouth, and he was stirring his hand through the slimy, wet mass of snails and singing a song. He winked lasciviously at the girls, which made them laugh. They wouldn't tell us what the song was about, but it was quite rude, apparently.

In the Gothic quarter, the girls took us to an old bar that Hemmingway used to frequent. Inside, it was cooler than the street, like an ancient, dark, sherry-smelling cave. I bet it hadn't changed for fifty years. My grandad and great Uncle had been in Barcelona in the 1930s as part of the International Brigade. I wondered if I was walking in their footsteps.

On the walls were ancient and colourful bullfighting posters, and over the bar was an enormous taxidermy head of a black Spanish fighting bull.

Isabel ordered cold, dry *fino* sherry for us all, and the waiter brought a large plate of fried and battered cuttle-fish for tapas. It was delicious. I thought that if I could make one day in my life last forever, then this would be the one I'd choose, with this beautiful girl beside me, holding my hand, and our best friends sitting next to us. It was perfect.

We walked the rest of the way down the Ramblas to the Columbus monument at Port Vell. I think Elena and I were averaging at least one kiss every twenty yards. We were crazy about each other. I recalled Tom's words about not getting too close, as we'd soon be saying goodbye, but it was too late for that. We'd both already decided this was only just the beginning.

We walked to La Segrada Familia, Gaudi's famous cathedral. It had been under construction for nearly a hundred years and was still only half-finished. It was breath-taking.

"Good job we don't take so long building a semi, Dan, or the old man would be bankrupt," Tom said.

"Yeah, long way to carry the hods, mate," I said, looking at the enormous towers on the front of the building.

We finished the evening in a tiny, backstreet tapas bar, then we walked back—tired, happy, and a bit drunk —to the *estacion*.

We caught the train and then the last bus from Blanes back to Lloret. The bus was full of late-night Barcelona revellers, heading back to the resorts. Elena rested her head on my shoulder as the bus rattled its way home. Tom and Isabel chatted and laughed together in the seats behind.

Back in Lloret, Tom walked Isabel home. Elena and I sat on a wall by the seafront, discussing what we were going to do when the holiday had ended. We both knew that we had to be together. Considering the vast distance that would soon be between us, though, our future together looked a bit challenging, to say the least.

Elena said she could come to England as soon as she was eighteen. Her parents wouldn't be able to stop her. Neither of us relished the thought of being apart for that long, though.

But I had an idea forming in my head. It was a stupid idea, perhaps, but dead simple.

Maybe it was just a dream, but as my old nan always told me, "You're better to have dreams than nightmares, son."

I walked her back to her aunt's house, and we kissed goodnight on the doorstep.

Elena hesitated a little and then said, "Do you want to meet my aunt tomorrow, Danny? If she meets you, she'll like you, and then when she speaks with *mi madre*, she'll tell her you're a nice boy. It would make things easier for us, maybe?"

My girlfriend had really thought this one through. She was smart.

I agreed. "Yes, I'd love to meet her."

I was secretly terrified at the prospect of meeting a Spanish aunt. I wasn't sure what to expect, but I'd got an image in my head of a sinister, black-clad, disapproving old woman who hated English boys. I hoped I was wrong. We arranged to meet after her class on Monday, and then we'd go back to her aunties for dinner.

I told Tom when I got back to the hotel.

"Bloody hell, Danny boy!" He laughed. "You're certainly getting your feet under the table. You really are serious about this girl, aren't you?"

I told him how we felt about each other, though I think he already knew anyway. Tom and I had been friends for too long to keep secrets from one another.

"Listen, mate," he said, she's a wonderful girl, and you'd be a fool not to want to be with her, but you live in

England, and she lives in northern Spain. It's not like you can pop 'round to see her on your Fizzy or take her to the pictures on a Saturday night, is it?"

"I know it sounds crazy, Tom," I replied, "and we haven't quite figured it out yet, but we're gonna be together somehow."

"Do you think her folks will let her come to England?" Tom asked.

"If they won't, then I'll go to Spain," I told him.

Tom looked me in the eye. He knew that once I'd made my mind up, there wasn't much chance of changing it. Suddenly, he looked a bit crestfallen. "What am I going to do if you go to Spain? You're my best mate. We've been best mates since we were little. I don't want to spend the rest of my life hanging around with Bullshit Dave."

With butterflies in my stomach and clutching a bunch of flowers for her auntie, I met Elena on Monday after class. We walked the half-mile to her aunt's apartment on a quiet back street. The flat was on the first floor up a flight of marble steps. Elena opened the door, and we walked into the hallway.

She called out, "Pili!"

A voice replied, "*Si, una momento.*"

We heard the sound of pots and pans rattling from the kitchen. Elena smiled at me. "She's cooking. *Mi tia* is always cooking."

Something certainly smelled delicious. "Mmm, hope it's snails," I said.

Elena showed me into the living room, which was bright and airy, with a balcony overlooking the street. A small, neat lady walked into the room. She wasn't wearing black but a light summer dress. She looked about forty or forty-five years old. She had brown hair tied back, and she bore a resemblance to her niece. Good looks and delicate features must run in the family.

Still holding my hand, Elena introduced us. "*Tia, este es* Daniel, *mi novio.*"

Her auntie smiled and held out her hand.

I handed her the bunch of flowers and said a little awkwardly, "*Encantado de conocerte,*" using the formal greeting that I'd found in my phrasebook.

Elena laughed, surprised. "Hey, you been practising, Danny?"

"Yes," I replied. "All morning."

Her auntie asked Elena if I could speak Spanish, and she told her that I was learning. Pili knew a little English from working in a gift shop in the town, and with her niece translating, we managed to talk well enough.

Her auntie asked about my family, my home, my work. She told me how she'd come to be in Lloret De Mar. Coincidentally, it was during a holiday in Lloret that she'd met her future husband on a day trip to Barcelona. Maybe this gave her some sympathy for mine and Elena's situation.

Elena's uncle was a Catalan called Jose. He turned up for dinner around one o'clock. Jose was a big guy with a ready smile. He was a crane driver, and in common with most of the southern Spanish building trade, he started his summertime working days at first light to be finished before the day got too hot. I sensed an ally in Jose, a kindred working man, and I instinctively liked him. I must admit, I'd expected to be treated with polite suspicion, but I think these people thought I was okay.

We talked about the recent trip to Barcelona. I told him my granddad and great uncle had been there as part of the International Brigade in the 1930s. Luckily for me, Jose was a republican.

As the dinnertime wine started to flow, I think they began to warm to me. Pili's dinner was delicious, and we talked and laughed a lot and drank more wine. Elena squeezed my hand under the table. I knew that she was glad that the meeting with her aunt and uncle was going so well.

Elena had confided to her aunt that we were serious about each other, and Pili asked us how we could possibly make a future together. I told her that somehow, I was going to get back to Albarracin to be with Elena, but what we were going to do after that, I didn't know. She just smiled at her husband and said something in Spanish.

Pedro (the mullet) called in on his way home from work to visit his mam and dad (and I guess check out his cousin's boyfriend). Initially, he treated me with suspicion—understandably, I supposed. An English tourist lusting over his pretty teenage cousin was always going to look a bit dodgy. Before long, though, we were getting on. He was an all right bloke. I decided that I should never judge a man by his hairstyle, no matter how outdated it was.

Elena walked to the corner of the street with me, and we arranged to meet the next day as usual. She was really pleased that I'd made a good impression on her family. Her mam and aunt were very close, and she was sure that Pili would be reporting back to her sister very soon. I walked back to the hotel in a reflective, happy state, marvelling at my situation. It seemed like ages since I'd left England to have a holiday with my best mate and his family, and now I'd just met the relatives of the girl I wanted to spend the rest of my life with. My life was getting surreal.

When I got back to our room, I told Tom all about the meeting with Elena's auntie. He'd had a bit of time to think things over. He came and sat on the edge of my bed and said, "Listen, Dan, we've been best mates all of our lives, and nothing's going to change that. I think you're doing the right thing. She's an amazing girl, and if you don't believe you can live without her, then you should follow your heart."

Though Tom and I joked a lot and took the piss out of each other constantly, he was always in my corner.

ELEVEN

The Tide Is High, But I'm Holding On

WE FINALLY GAVE in to Sue's curiosity and invited the girls out for dinner to meet her and Phil. We all met up at a little restaurant on the seafront, though Trudy and Kim declined the invitation. Speaking for both herself and Kim, Trudy said, "Spanish food was too greasy for them. And besides, it makes your breath smell like a badger's arse and gives you spots."

The sheer inventiveness of this girl's vocabulary never failed to amaze us.

"That girl! I don't know where she gets her language from. It must be your side of the family," Sue said, frowning at Phil. "Bloody builders!" she added, laughing.

Phil and Sue really enjoyed holidays in Spain and the livelier the resort, the better, they loved the beach, the discos and bars, and they even seemed to like the slightly tacky entertainment at the hotel. The bands, the plastic Elvis impersonator and the Spanish Roy Orbison singing 'Preety Woman,' Everything here was so different from England, the beer was cold, and the sea was warm, the sky was blue, the sun shone continuously, and there was plenty of building sites to look at in case Phil got homesick.

Elena and Isabel arrived, turning heads as they walked into the restaurant. Tom and I had been looking out for them, and we waved, they spotted us and headed for our table, I noticed Sue raise her eyebrows and glance at her husband. These girls were something else, dazzling smiles, long shining hair, slim and beautiful, both wearing calf-length skirts and tight tops with silver bangles jingling on their wrists. Individually they were enchanting, but together they were stunning.

They sat down a little shyly next to Sue on the opposite side of the table to Tom, Phil, and me. We introduced our girlfriends to Tom's parents.

Big Phil was in his element, kissing their hands and using bad Spanish. "*Encantardy, encantardy, senoritas.*" I could see where Tom had got the charming bullshit gene from.

He ordered a big jug of sangria, and the waiter brought it to the table along with the usual sparklers and small complimentary glasses of peach Schnapps. Sitting opposite Elena, I couldn't keep my eyes off her; she was just so perfect. Sue and the girls got on well immediately and seeing them sitting and chatting together; they could all have been nearly the same age. I don't think the girls could believe that Sue was old enough to be Tom and Trudy's mam.

Phil winked at Tom and me and said under his breath, "Aye up, lads. Bloody hell, batting a bit above your average with these two, ain't you?" He was obviously impressed.

It was a beautiful evening, and we sat at a table overlooking the beach across the street, where it was still hot enough for people to be lying on the sand. It was that early evening lull when the British sun worshippers had gone back to their hotels to dab after sun or calamine lotion on their peeling red skin, drink cold beer and get ready for their 'peak too early' nights out in the town.

The much more sensible Spanish holiday makers traditionally cleared off the beach before the fierce midday heat kicked in and headed back for the gentler evening rays before sunset. Their children were still playing in the surf and kicking footballs around. The Spanish wouldn't be hitting the bars and discos en masse, till eleven PM at the earliest, by which time most of the British, finding themselves liberated from the UK's strict licensing laws, would be staggering around singing 'Viva Espana' at the top of their lungs and throwing up in the ashtrays.

The girls were making a great impression on Tom's parents. We told them of Trudy's meeting with Elena and Isabel, and we recounted the conversation between them both.

"Our Trudy is a little minx. I'm so sorry, girls," said Phil, laughing.

In his eyes, though, Trudy could never do any wrong. She was perfect. He adored his spirited, cheeky daughter. We all did, really, even though she could be a right pain sometimes.

Sue chipped in, "She's all right, really, girls. Just

don't let her bully you. Give her as good as you get, and you'll be okay. You can say what you want about our Trude, though. There's never a dull moment when she's around."

I don't know how much of the conversation the Spanish girls were understanding. Sue did speak quite fast, and with a strong local accent, especially when she'd had a few bevvies. As the drink flowed and the conversation became more relaxed, the girls offered to take Sue shopping to Barcelona before the end of the holiday, and Sue and Phil said they'd love to come camping in Albarracin sometime. Though to be honest, people always say that sort of thing on holiday when they've had a few drinks, and I didn't think Sue would make a great camper. She was a tough enough kind of lady, but I couldn't see her sitting on an upturned bucket, eating baked beans out of a tin. As for Trudy, living in a tent with her for two weeks was just too horrible to contemplate.

Sue looked at the four of us sitting at the table, sighed, and said, "It's such a shame that you'll all be saying goodbye soon. You look like you're made for each other. Never mind, though, you can keep in touch and maybe meet up again next year."

I said quite seriously, "Oh, don't worry, Sue. Elena and I aren't saying goodbye for long. We're going to be together again soon."

Sue smiled at me across the table, reached over and patted my hand. "Of course, Danny, love. I'm sure you'll sort something out."

But I didn't think for a minute that she believed we ever would.

The night out with Tom's parents was loads of fun, and I hoped that Sue and Phil would tell my folks all about Elena when we got home and how lovely she is. I still had to keep pinching myself and telling myself that it was all real, my beautiful girlfriend, the beach, even the restaurant with the sparklers and the cocktails- Legovers, Harvey Wallbangers, and Fuzzy Navels. It all seemed terribly sophisticated and mind-blowingly extravagant to me. I was from the land of warm bitter and lager and lime, faggots and peas and bingo at the working men's club, my idea of tapas was a pickled egg dropped into a bag of crisps by a taciturn barman with dubious personal hygiene standards. Or a limp bag of prawns from the man who carried the huge wicker basket of seafood around the local pubs and clubs on a Saturday night.

"Aye up, mate, got any mussels?" We'd shout to him.

"Sure," he'd reply.

"Well, why aren't you carrying two baskets then?"

Every week, the same joke. We never tired of it. I wondered what the steward at our local working men's club would have said if we'd asked him for a sparkler in our pints of Double Diamond.

We all walked back along the seafront to the hotel for the nightly entertainment. The three girls walked together in front, arm in arm across the *paseo*, talking and laughing. Tom, Phil, and I trailed along behind them, smoking, chatting, all three of us watching the three incredibly attractive women walking upfront. Tom and I would sooner have taken the girls somewhere else, a nightclub or disco, but Elena and Isabel were getting on well with Tom's parents, and they wanted to see our hotel. Tonight's entertainment was the house disco and a Spanish band, two cute girl singers with mad Afro perms, and a few mullety musicians with the obligatory 'Gringo' moustaches, playing mainly English pop tunes. Sue and the girls dragged me, Phil, and Tom onto the dance floor.

Oh, God, I thought. *This is when she finds out I dance like an out of control gibbon.*

I really concentrated and tried to make my legs behave themselves and not start freelancing independently from my brain as they usually did after a few drinks. Miraculously, though, tonight, they seemed to be conforming. Looking around me, I could see Tom dancing with Isabel like they owned the dancefloor, and there were lots of middle-aged men 'dad dancing' with their wives.

Some of them, Phil included, were exhibiting some quite extraordinarily ridiculous footwork. For a change, I felt quite cool. I think I'd gotten away with it.

Later, Elena and I managed to slip off to mine and Tom's room to be alone for a little while, but Trudy and Kim came bursting in next door with some of their new, rowdy friends making a lot of noise and banging on the wall, so it kind of ruined the mood a bit.

We'd been making plans. Elena had bought a map and as far as we could see it was about 1200-1300 miles from my village in the Midlands to Albarracin, probably a lot more on a moped as you couldn't use the motorways on a 50cc bike so I'd have to stick to the smaller roads. I wasn't sure if a well-used Fizzy could travel that far, but I figured if I went steady and did maybe 100-150 miles a day, then I could probably do it in seven-to-ten days. I could take my tent and find somewhere to pitch it at night. I'd be fine if the weather stayed good and the bike didn't break down. Elena usually worked on the campsite reception in the evenings, and this was where the family's only telephone was, except for a payphone outside. I could phone her every few days and tell her of my progress. I think I'd got just about enough money left in my post office savings account for the ferry, fuel, food, and campsites. I'd have to kiss goodbye to any thoughts of getting a bigger bike, but that didn't bother me, we'd at least got a plan, even if it was a bit half-arsed.

When I got back to England, I figured it would take me a couple of weeks to get the Fizzy prepared, and everything else sorted out for the journey. I'd have to give Phil two weeks' notice, but the fortnight's wages would top up my travelling fund. We didn't have a clue what we were going to do when I got to Spain, but it didn't matter that much to us. As long as we were together, we weren't worried about anything else. We were kids, ridiculously optimistic and completely crazy about each other. Being together all seemed so perfectly simple, and we thought everything else would just sort itself out.

We were desperate to spend a night together before the end of the holiday, and we thought we could maybe scrape enough money together between the two of us for a room in a hostel in one of the nearby resorts. Elena could tell her auntie she was stopping at Isabel's, she sometimes stayed there anyway, and I wouldn't be missed at the hotel. We didn't like lying to people, but we both knew that this was our last few days together for a while, and we didn't want to miss a single second of them. Elena booked the room the next day at a pension in Pineda that we'd found in the phonebook, they were very busy, but they'd had a cancellation. We were a newly married couple, passing through town on our way to Almeria for our honey-moon, she told the lady on the other end of the phone. I was amazed. It was a revelation to find out that teenage girls were just as horny and devious as teenage boys.

I told Tom of our plan and, ever resourceful, he said he'd ask Isabel if she could stay at the hotel for the night. She could work the old double bluff on her folks and say she was staying the night at Elena's aunt's. Both of the girls could head straight for the language school in the morning, and nobody would be any the wiser. The plan seemed watertight, and we gave ourselves a little pat on the back.

The hostel was a tall, slightly tired looking Venetian style building with iron Juliet balconies overlooking the road. It was two streets back from the seafront. The reception was marble tiled, cool, airy, and suggested the place had seen wealthier times. We checked in, Elena flashing a gold ring she'd borrowed from Isabel, I kept my ringless hand firmly in my pocket, and my mouth shut. I doubt if the lady at the reception believed a word of it, but she handed us the key with a raised eyebrow and wished us goodnight.

We ran up the stairs giggling like children. I was carrying my small, battered suitcase, which we'd brought as a prop, along with a bottle of cheap Spanish wine. We unlocked the shabby, brown painted door to paradise.

I woke the next morning to see her beautiful eyes looking right into mine. I don't think I'd ever been so deliriously happy in my whole life, and I think she felt the same, but we were naive. We didn't know how fleetingly fickle happiness could be.

We kissed goodbye on the corner of the street by the language school and made plans to meet later in the afternoon.

I stood and watched her trim little figure walk down the road. I got butterflies in my stomach just from looking at her. She turned, waved, smiled, and blew me a kiss before she disappeared through the door.

Back in the hotel, I found Tom in the dining room, having breakfast.

"All right, mate?"

"Yeah, okay, Dan. How'd you get on?" he replied with a raised eyebrow.

"We had a lovely night, mate," I said with a massive grin on my face. "How did things go with the lovely Isabel?"

"No go, mate. I'm afraid she wouldn't stay the night.

She said she was known by some of the hotel staff who were friends of her dad's and ex-employees from the cinema. It was just too risky if someone saw her creeping out in the morning."

I told him all about the night before, though I left out the more intimate bits. We used to share all of the gory details of our clumsy encounters but being with Elena was almost sacred. It didn't seem right to tell anybody, not even my best mate.

"You'd better get some breakfast, you stud, before you waste away." He laughed, grabbing me in a head-lock and knuckling my head.

"We've got two days left before we head home. We'd better make the most of it, son."

We were meeting the girls at the usual place after class, so we swam, sunbathed, and kicked a football around on the beach with some of the other lads from the hotel before heading up to the bar. I'd been thinking about my girlfriend for every second of the day since we'd kissed goodbye that morning. It was almost agony waiting to see her again. I was like a junkie needing a fix.

The girls were late. I was starting to feel a little nagging worry in the pit of my stomach.

We spotted Isabel running up the street, and she sat down breathlessly at our table. She looked upset. Looking at me, she started talking rapidly in Spanish and then seeing my blank expression, she checked herself and started speaking in English.

Elena's father had phoned Pili's apartment to talk to his daughter last night. It was an important message.

Her grandfather had taken ill, and they were short-handed at the campsite. He wanted her to get on a train and come home as soon as possible. Pili had given him Isabel's telephone number, and he'd phoned her apartment to speak with Elena.

You can guess the rest.

Her dad had driven through the night and picked his daughter up from the school. Her case was already packed and in the boot of his car. They'd be well on their way back to the north by now. I felt as if someone had kicked me in the guts. If I hadn't been sitting down, I would have fallen down. I must have looked crestfallen because Tom leaned over and squeezed my shoulder.

"Come on, mate. Don't worry. It won't change anything. You'll be back with her before you know it. I can see the headlines now; *Lovesick, spotty English kid crosses Pyrenees on a Fizzy*." He was only trying to make me laugh, but I don't think I had a laugh left in me.

He went inside to get me a brandy, and Isabel lit me a cigarette. I asked Isabel if Elena had given her a message for me, but she said it all happened so quickly that she didn't get the chance, her friend's dad was waiting outside the school, and he just told his daughter to get in the car. Isabel said he didn't look so happy.

I dashed into a shop, bought a postcard, and wrote a message to Elena, Isabel got me a stamp and mailed it for me, it should reach Elena in two or three days she said.

I tried to phone her that evening, but the phone on the campsite reception was answered by somebody who hung up on me as soon as they heard an English voice asking for Elena.

Tom put things into perspective later. "You can't blame her dad, mate, he tries to reach his daughter, and she's out with some English tourist after telling her auntie that she's staying at her friend's house. It does look a bit dodgy, doesn't it? Don't worry, Dan, as soon as her parents meet you, they'll like you. At the moment, though, you're just some shady English character who wants to lead their daughter astray."

He was right, and even though I was cross and hurt, I could see the logic in what he was saying. I guess we'd been idiots spending the night at the hostel at a time when we should have been trying to impress people rather than pissing them off. British parents would maybe have shrugged it off and chalked it up to normal teenage behaviour. This was my first stark lesson in the cultural differences between the catholic Spanish and the Brits. In our defence, though, we were young and completely crazy about each other.

"It wasn't our fault. It was the fucking hormones," I told Tom.

"Try telling her old fella that," he said wryly, "I'm sure he'll understand."

On our last day, Tom spent most of the time with Isabel, and I mostly stayed at the hotel, chain-smoking cigarettes and drinking beer, sullen and moping around feeling very sorry for myself. I tried to call Elena from the payphone in the lobby, but again somebody hung up on me. I felt completely helplessness and frustrated, she was gone, and for the time being there wasn't a thing I could do about it. There was a horrible, empty churning in my stomach. I was going 'cold turkey' without my girlfriend, and it was sickening. I made up my mind that I was going to start my journey back to Spain within two weeks of getting home. I could maybe get back to her in less than a month.

Trudy and Kim were next door, probably getting ready to go out, I heard them singing 'Puppy Love', loudly and tunelessly.

Once again, I marvelled at how such pretty girls could sound so horrible.

I know the old Donny Osmond tear-jerker was directed at me, normally I'd have laughed, but I still wasn't feeling much like laughing.

Tom came back at around ten PM. He'd walked Isabel home and said goodbye to her. He wasn't too upset, they'd got on well, but they were more like best mates when they were together, laughing, joking, dancing. They were going to keep in touch, but it wasn't a 'love job' like Elena and me. He persuaded me to go downstairs for a drink, where Phil and Sue were spending the last night of the holidays. Everybody was there, including Trudy and Kim, they were all having a laugh, making the most of our last night in Spain.

I felt a bit ashamed of myself for being so sullen, and after a couple of drinks, I started to feel a bit more optimistic. No point in moping around, I decided I was going to pull myself together and make my own destiny.

"C'mon, Danny. Let's have a dance," said Sue, standing up and holding out her hand to me.

"Do you know what you're letting yourself in for, mam?" said Trudy. "He ain't exactly Lionel Blair, you know."

"I know, Trude," Sue replied with a sigh, "but someone's gotta dance with the poor little bugger. Look at him, sat sitting there all lost and lovelorn."

I laughed and followed Sue onto the dance floor. You couldn't stay sad for very long with these people around you, they were fantastic.

We had a late afternoon flight home the next day, so I had time in the morning to go and see Elena's Tia Pili. I'd written down a few things in Spanish that I wanted to say to her, using my dictionary and with some help from one of the hotel waiters that we'd befriended who was sympathetic towards my shattered love life.

Pili answered the door and asked me inside the apartment. She made coffee, and we sat on her balcony.

I tried to explain to her that I was sorry about what we'd done and that we didn't like to lie to her, but we were just so desperate to be together. I told her that I was going to be heading out to Albarracin in two weeks and nobody was going to stop Elena and me from being together. I think maybe she was a little bit surprised that I'd visited her. Perhaps she'd started to believe that I was just a chancer who wanted to sleep with her pretty niece and then disappear. I pleaded with her to talk to Elena's mam, and tell her that I wasn't such a bad guy. I think she could see I was upset, and as I was leaving, she squeezed my hand and promised me she'd phone her sister and talk with her. I thanked her and told her I hoped I'd see her and Jose again.

Back at the hotel, Tom and I packed our cases and went down to the bar to wait for everybody. We sat at a table with a last beer before the coach came to take us to Girona.

"It's been a fantastic holiday, Dan," said my mate, I know you've had a bit of a rough time these last couple of days, but you've enjoyed yourself, haven't you?"

"Enjoyed myself?" I answered. "God, mate! I've had the best time of my life, ever."

"Me too," said Tom. "It's been brilliant. I'm gonna miss Isabel. I guess I liked her a bit more than I thought I did."

"Isabel's lovely, mate," I replied, then I laughed. "Two weeks ago, we were going to be gigolos."

"Are you still dead set on coming back?" Tom asked me.

"Yes, mate," I replied. "I'm going to start out in two weeks and try to get back to Elena before August's out."

"Our Trude ain't gonna be happy, you know."

"Aww c'mon, mate," I replied. "Trudy doesn't care anything about me. She just uses me to impress her little school friends."

Tom just looked at me with a raised eyebrow. Right then, the rest of our party appeared in the bar carrying suitcases and bags, Kim and Trudy wearing the obligatory straw sombreros. Ten minutes later, we were on the coach driving to the airport.

From thirty-five thousand feet, I looked through the cabin window at the massive expanse of parched farmland; neat, crosshatched olive groves; and vast mountains below us. We were heading north-west. I wondered if we were flying over Albarracin. My stomach lurched as I thought about the vast, ever-increasing distance between my girl and myself. I wondered if she was looking up at vapour trails in the sky and thinking about me.

TWELVE

I Am The Upsetter

It DIDN'T SEEM to be very long before we were descending through the grey blanket of cloud that was wrapping the British Isles like a shroud this year, Spain already seemed a million miles away…

Last summer, 1976, had been a scorcher. Tom and I had been working on his dad's building sites, and we'd got ourselves Hollywood suntans, nearly everybody got a suntan in the summer of '76. Despite missing my girlfriend, I was glad to be home, I was looking forward with excited trepidation to seeing my folks and my brother and telling them all about Spain and Elena. I really wasn't looking forward to explaining my plans to my mam and dad, though. I thought my dad would be okay, but my mam—well that could be tricky. At least Sue and Phil had met Elena, so they'd be able to tell my parents how wonderful she was, and mam and dad wouldn't think I'd gone completely off my rocker.

More than anything, I was keen to start working on

my bike and getting everything sorted and ready for the journey back to Spain.

Kim and Trudy were comparing suntans on the way home in the car. They couldn't wait to show themselves off to their pasty-faced friends who'd spent the Leicester fortnight shivering in Skegness or Mablethorpe.

"Now you've tanned up, you look a bit Spanish, Trude," said Kim.

"Like a gormless old mare, d'you mean?" Trudy replied, pulling a face, digging me in the ribs and laughing.

I didn't rise to the bait.

I had to admit, though, they both looked pretty good. They'd spent every available moment working on their tans and even at the hottest times of the day when the sun was unbearable, they'd been on the beach, lying in the sun, soaking up the rays like cats. The girls still had a few weeks of summer holiday left before they started the next school term, so they were happy. Tom and I had one day to acclimate before we were back on site, and I needed to tell Phil that I'd only be working for him for another couple of weeks. I had lots of difficult things to tell people, and I wasn't looking forward to it.

Phil pulled up outside our house, and I thanked him and Sue for the wonderful holiday. My mam, seeing Phil's car, popped out to say hello.

"Has he been a good little boy, Sue?" She asked, hugging me and laughing.

"No, he's been a little sod," Sue replied, "they've been up to all sorts of shenanigans, all four of them."

My mam kissed me, right there in the street, Tom,

Kim, and Trudy howled with laughter. I slung them a big 'vee' sign and mouthed an obscenity.

"See you up the cross later, Tom," I added.

I waved goodbye to them, I was home, after leaving Spain just a few hours ago. It seemed strange to be standing outside of our house with my mam. It was great to be home, but I wished I could afford to buy an airline ticket and fly straight back to Spain. That was way beyond my means though. The only way I could do that was if I sold my bike and rinsed out my post office savings account. But, I guess I was going to need transport if I wanted to find work when I got to Albarracin.

Spain didn't seem that far away when you'd just stepped off an aeroplane.

Now for the hard part: telling my mam and dad. I thought I'd perhaps put the task off for a couple of days while I worked on my pitch. Meanwhile, I was desperate to speak to Elena. I got through to the campsite reception again from the callbox in the village, but when I asked for Elena, a man answered and said she wasn't there—at least that's what I thought he said, (no esta aqui).

Back on site Monday morning, Phil had told the lads about some of the highlights of the holiday, and predictably they were ripping the piss out of Tom and me regarding our foray into 'alternative' Spanish nightlife, but we expected it and took it in good humour.

I'd told Phil that I was going back to Spain and I wanted to work a fortnight's notice. Phil was a patient man. He just said, "think about it, lad, talk to your mam and dad first, see how you feel in a couple of weeks."

The jungle drums had been beating. Sue must have mentioned Elena to my folks because that evening, my mam asked me about 'my little holiday romance.' I told her I'd met a wonderful girl, and it wasn't just a 'little holiday romance.'

I'd been desperate to look at the photos I'd taken of Elena. I wanted so badly to see her face again. There was a chemist's shop in town that developed pictures in twenty-four hours, so I'd taken my rolls of film in as soon as possible, and I collected them on Tuesday during my dinner break. Resisting the temptation to tear open the envelope full of prints in the shop, I rode back to work as fast as I could. In the site hut with Tom, I feverishly tore open the packet, and we looked at the photos. I hadn't imagined it. She really was the most gorgeous girl I'd ever seen.

As we sat around the kitchen table after tea on Tuesday, I showed the photos to my family. I passed the pictures around —Jim first, then my mam and dad. Jim thumbed through the pile of prints, remarking on the blue sky and the beach, the hotel, and the Barcelona landmarks... until he came to the first picture of Elena. She was on the beach, her brown skin contrasting with the yellow bikini she was wearing. It was my favourite photo. She looked amazing.

"Wow! Is this your girl, our kid?" he remarked, his eyes nearly popping out of his head. "Has she got a sister?"

"That's Elena, mate," I replied. "She's got a big sister, but 'fraid she's married."

Jim handed the photo to my mam.

"Oh, Daniel, she's just beautiful," said my mam, squinting at the picture. "Sue said she was pretty. She's very Spanish, isn't she? Does she do Flamenco dancing?"

My mam hadn't travelled much. She wasn't knowledgeable about foreign people and cultures. The extent of her knowledge of international lifestyles came from *Alan whicker* or the *Wish You Were Here* TV show. I think she expected all Spanish girls to carry castanets in their handbags and break into wild gypsy dancing at the drop of a sombrero. A couple of years ago, Tom had a French foreign exchange student stay for a week, he was a small spotty boy with braces on his teeth, my mam had been quite disappointed that he didn't look like Charles Aznavour and wear a beret.

My dad put his specs on and looked at the picture, then raised his eyebrows. Doing his best Peter Cook impersonation, he said in a deadpan voice, "The Iberian Peninsula does produce some extraordinarily beautiful women. I used to carry a bit of a torch for Carmen Miranda, you know. Though, I never went a bundle on all that fruit stuck on top of her head. More of a veg man myself."

Staying in character, he carried on: "Now if she'd had a nice bit of broccoli stuck on top of her noggin or a fresh Savoy cabbage then I possibly would have left your mother for her."

At this, my mam grabbed a cauliflower out of the vegetable rack in the corner of the kitchen and holding it on her head, she started dancing around the room.

"How 'bout this, you daft old git, is this doing it for you?"

"Don't know about him, but it's certainly doing it for me, Sal," said our milkman, Alf, who'd just appeared at the open kitchen door to collect the milk money.

We all fell about laughing. There was always a lot of laughter in our house. I was going to miss these people, but I'd got to tell them my plan; I'd been putting it off for three days now. My mouth seemed to be on autopilot when I blurted out, "Mam, Dad, I'm going back to Spain."

"Of course, love," said my mam. "I bet you miss her, don't you? But don't worry. If you save your money, you can go back next summer and see her again."

"No, mam, I'm going back soon, in a couple of weeks even. I'm going to ride out there on my bike."

There was an uneasy silence for a few seconds until my mam laughed out loud. "Daniel, you do have some crazy ideas in your head. What are you going to do in Spain? How would you make a living?"

"I thought I'd learn to play the guitar, mam. Elena and I could go around the bars as a double act. She could dance and I could play Flamenco music," I replied with more than a little sarcasm.

"You can't ride to Spain on a moped Daniel," my dad reasoned, "not for a girl you just met on holiday."

"She's not 'just a girl,' dad," I said. "She's *the* girl, and of course you can ride to Spain on a moped. Can't you, Jim?" I turned to my big brother for back up.

"Well, I suppose you could ride to Spain on a

moped," said Jim thoughtfully. "You just wouldn't get there very quickly."

"Don't encourage him, James, for God's sake. I thought you had more sense?" said my mam.

And with that, and expecting trouble, Jim excused himself and slipped out to the garage to tinker with his motorbike. Jim was a nice fellow and an ally, but he liked the quiet life.

I was okay though, I'd anticipated this conversation for the last week, and I'd got plenty of ammo in the arsenal ready to fire back.

"Dad, you told me that you fell in love with Mam the minute you clapped eyes on her. You told me that you knew right from the start that she was the only girl for you. Would you have ridden to Spain on a moped for her?"

"Of course, I would've, son," my dad replied, slightly flustered. "I'd have crawled to Spain over broken glass for her, but that's different."

"No, it isn't, Dad. There's no difference, and don't tell me I'm just a kid either, cause you were only sixteen when you met Mam."

With a raised eyebrow, he looked over the table at my mam for help. He couldn't really argue with that though, I'd snookered him. I picked up my crash helmet and walked out of the back door.

"Dan and Trudy are going to be upset," was my mam's parting shot.

I loved these people, but I knew this was going to be a battle of wits, and I felt like I'd just won the first round.

I rode up to the cross to meet Tom, him and Trudy were both sitting on the wall eating chips. They often used to eat chips for tea, their dad did too. Sue was a lovely mother and a fantastic wife, and they all loved her, but she was a terrible cook, her food was tragic. My mam had taught her some quite simple meals to cook for the family, but Sue usually made a mess of things. She desperately wanted to be a good cook. She devoured cookery books, and she always watched '*The Galloping Gourmet*' on TV with a pen and notebook in hand, writing down the recipes feverishly. She'd attempt some quite ambitious dishes, but they nearly always went wrong, and you'd often find Phil in the chippy at teatime. Sue Green's culinary disasters were common knowledge, and when he was queueing in the chip shop, his friends would often ask him, "Hi, Phil. What did she cook for tea?"

"Coq au vin, or tomato and tuna en gelee," he'd reply with a little shudder before ordering himself haddock and chips to eat in the beer garden of The White Lion.

It'd be several decades before microwave ovens, pre-prepared meals, and YouTube tutorials would be available. Meanwhile, the family were quite used to over-cooked elaborate party food and the occasional 'Vesta' curry or burnt Fray Bentos pie. Phil would have to wait until 1990 before 'Chicken Tonight' launched their ready-made sauces and Sue would finally manage to knock up a Coq au vin without endangering life.

As I pulled up at the Cross, Tom and Trudy looked up from their chips and batter bits.

"All right, mate, how's it hanging?" Said Tom.

"Ok, mate," I replied, "I just told mam and dad that I was going back to Spain, so things are a bit rocky at home at the moment."

"What do you mean, going back to Spain?" said Trudy abruptly, looking at me, puzzled, her brow furrowed. I suddenly realised how stupid I'd been, but it was too late now.

"I'm going back to Spain, Trude, on my bike. I thought you knew."

"What, next summer?"

"No, in a couple of weeks."

Tom and I changed the subject and chatted awkwardly. Both of us were aware that we were sitting very close to an unexploded bomb. Trudy didn't say anything. She just sat quietly for a couple of minutes, staring at the tarmac, drumming her platform heels on the brick wall. Then she stood up, screwed her chip bag into a ball and threw it at me, point-blank range. Chips and batter bits exploded in my face, and a chorus of applause and laughter rang out from the other kids sitting on the wall.

"You can't ride to Spain on your moped, Daniel, YOU TWAT!" She shouted, choking back tears, before turning around and running off down the road.

"What the fuck's up with your sister, mate?" I asked Tom incredulously while I picked bits of batter from my hair.

"I think you know what's up with her, Dan, don't you? I think she likes you, mate," he replied quite seriously with his eyebrow raised.

I felt a knot in my stomach—another knot to put with the one that Elena had left there.

Trudy meant the world to me. She'd been like my little sister, and her reaction really shook me. I should have spoken to her first and broken the news gently rather than just blurting it out matter-of-factly. She was usually tough, tomboyish, and independent, but suddenly she seemed vulnerable. I'd never seen her like that before. Tom and I went and sat at the top of the park, passing a cigarette between us.

"I didn't ever want to upset Trudy mate."

"I know, Dan. She's growing up. I think she's started to realise she likes you, and she doesn't want things to change. Nobody does," he added.

I'd made Trudy cry, and I felt like crap. It was going to be so hard to say goodbye to my best friends.

Next day, after work, I went into the garage and dug out the original handlebars for the bike. I'd fitted dropped, racing style 'Ace' bars, but I thought I'd be better off with the standard Sit Up and Beg ones. They'd be a lot more comfortable for the long journey ahead. I also found the chrome rack that had been on the bike when I first bought it. I bolted it back on. Jim walked into the garage. He'd recently succumbed to the lure of higher purchase and bought himself a brand-new Suzuki "Kettle," on the 'never never.' The 750cc water-cooled superbike that every biker kid wanted in the 1970s.

It sat at the far end of the garage—a beautiful red and chrome star ship of a bike that looked like it was doing a hundred miles an hour even when it was on its stand.

"I got you some new points, Danny. We'll give the Fizzy a service," he said, reaching for the toolbox.

"By the way, mate, I heard George and Mildred talking. [our nickname for our folks] They don't expect you to get much farther than Dover. I think they've decided to humour you for the time being."

"What do you think, Jim? Do you think I'll make it to Spain?" I asked my brother.

"Yeah, course you will. Just go steady, keep your wits about you, and watch out for those Frenchie drivers. They usually drive with one hand on the horn button and the other one on their girlfriend's knee."

Jim and a couple of his mates had been camping in France the previous summer on their bikes, and they hadn't been overly impressed by French drivers.

"Anyway, mate, she looks like she's worth it. Are you sure her sister's married?"

A little later, my dad walked through the garage door, he nodded at the bike, "You're going to need a top box for that rack, son. Keep your stuff safe. I've got some half-inch plywood. I'll start cutting it."

Half an hour later, looking slightly flustered, my mam stuck her head around the garage door and said urgently, "Danny, your girlfriend's on the phone."

I dropped my spanner and ran into the house.

"She sounds very nice," said my mam, as I ran through the kitchen to the small hallway at the bottom of the stairs where our trimphone sat on a white wrought iron and glass shelf.

I picked up the phone, "*Hola*, Elena. Are you okay? I've missed you so much." I couldn't get my words out quick enough.

"Are you coming back, Danny?" She sounded as desperate as me.

"*Si, claro*," I replied. "I start travelling at the end of next week. I'm fixing the moto for the journey."

We spoke only very briefly. Phone calls abroad were costly in the 1970s, and she'd promised her mam she'd talk for no more than a couple of minutes. Her grandad had suffered a heart attack, but he was recovering well, and her dad had been pretty cross about our hostel stunt, but he'd cooled down a bit now. Best of all, she told me she loved me, she missed me, and if I didn't come back to Spain, then she'd come to England.

Things were busy, and she was working every evening at the reception desk. We arranged that I'd phone her there when I was on the road. I felt elated and relieved. I slipped out of the front door so that my mam couldn't stop me in the kitchen and ask me any daft questions. I nearly floated back out to the garage.

"How's Carmen?" said my dad.

"She's terrific," I replied, "she couldn't speak for long because she was out of breath on account of all the 'Fandangoing'."

We all laughed. My dad was cutting the timber for my top box, and Jim had fitted my new points. I picked up the old set and started flatting the electrodes on a whetstone. They'd do for spares on the road.

"Who's for a beer?" Asked dad, he went to the kitchen and came back with three bottles of the foul-tasting brew. Jim and I pulled a face at each other, but we drank it all the same.

The next ten days flew by, Tom and I visited our usual haunts, and I worked all the hours I could. I still needed to get enough cash together to fund the journey. We made one final trip out together on our bikes, to Skegness, or 'Leicester-on-sea' as we called it, the east coast resort, a hundred miles up the road from us. Tom and I rode out to 'chapel point' a few miles from Skeggy, and I showed him the house I stayed in once when I was a child. It was one of a handful of bungalows across the street from the sea wall. My paternal grandad's brother, my great uncle Chris, and his wife aunty Kath had lived in one of these houses, and when I was eight years old, they invited me to stay with them for a summer holiday. My grandad—who lived two doors away from us—had warned me that his brother could be crotchety and mean, but the lure of a couple of weeks by the seaside, penny arcades, funfairs and sticks of rock had swayed my decision.

Uncle Chris and my grandad had been raised apart. My grandad had spent his early life in the rough and tumble dockside environment of the East end of London. His brother, Chris, had caught scarlet fever and was sent to relatives in Yorkshire to convalesce on a remote farm in the Dales. Chris had grown up differently to his brother. My Grandad was warm, funny, and generous. Uncle Chris was taciturn, grumpy, and tight-fisted. Aunty Kath, though, childless and maternal, had always been kind and welcoming to my brother and me.

Beside the bungalow, at the end of their driveway

was an old asbestos garage and next to that a caravan which Chris rented out to Butlins as high season over-spill accommodation for 'Redcoats' who worked at the nearby holiday camp. At the time I was there, it was occupied by two attractive girls in their late teens- early twenties, who went to work every morning dressed in their smart red uniforms.

The girls used the bathroom in the bungalow, and I once inadvertently burst through the door as one of the girls was standing naked on the bathroom mat, drying herself with a towel. She had pert breasts and an intriguing triangle of auburn hair between her legs. I stood transfixed, staring, not knowing whether to run away or continue gawping like a fool. She looked up and smiled, made no attempt to cover herself up, and just said, "Hello, cheeky. If you're coming in, shut the door behind you."

I stammered my apologies and ran out of the room, headlong into my uncle in the passageway. He later quizzed me on what I'd seen, but I denied the old pervert the pleasure of a description and told him the girl was wrapped in her towel.

My uncle's neighbours wanted a couple of tons of topsoil moving from their front driveway and barrowing to their back garden. Uncle Chris had kindly volunteered me for the job, and I spent several days of my holiday at the backbreaking task. When the job was finished, and my hands were blistered from shovelling, my uncle told aunty Kath that I'd worked like a 'Navvy.' The neighbours gave me a few shillings to spend in the arcades and probably rubbed their hands together at the bargain-basement labour rate they'd paid.

As a treat, and probably feeling a bit guilty, aunty Kath took me to Skegness to see a comedy show starring my 'Carry On' film hero, Sid James. After the show, we went to the stage door and joined the queue of fans waiting to get his autograph. He appeared wearing a red silk dressing gown and a paisley cravat, warm, affable, and larger than life, his leathery face creased in a smile and his eyes twinkled as he shook my hand and wrote on a publicity photo, "To Daniel, best wishes and keep on laughing." A few seconds out of the great man's life, but a magical moment that would stay with me forever. We walked back to the bus stop, eating chips, and talking about the show.

A few days later I was swimming in the sea with another boy my age who I'd met on the beach. Before I knew what was happening, the water had become very deep, and I was struggling to make my way back to the shore. I felt a breaker under my feet and tried to use it to shin along to get back to safety, but the undertow around these timbers was fearsome, and I was dragged under several times as if by invisible hands. I remember murky green water in front of my eyes, time and time again as I struggled with the riptide.

From nowhere, a man in a white rubber bathing hat grabbed me and pulled me to the surface. Swimming on our backs, he hauled me to the beach where he left me with the family of the boy I'd met. He disappeared before anybody could thank him. My legs were cut and bleeding from the sharp barnacles on the timbers, and I was coughing up foul-tasting lungfuls of the North Sea. The boy's mother wrapped me in a towel and helped me back over the sea wall to the bungalow, where my aunty Kath cleaned my cuts with surgical spirits, a fate almost as bad as drowning.

I don't know who my guardian angel in the white bathing hat was, but he undoubtedly saved my life and then slipped off without a word. I never told my parents or anybody about the incident, and neither did my aunty or Uncle—for fear of being accused of lax care I guessed. I told my mam the cuts on my legs were from a breaker, which wasn't a lie. The experience left me traumatised and a little afraid of water for my whole life. Tom was the only person I'd ever told this story to, as we sat on the seafront at Chapel point, eating fish and chips.

It was low tide, and I pointed out the mean, gnarly old breaker that had nearly killed me eight years before, I Kung Fu kicked it and threw a stone at it in contempt. The pebble ricocheted off the ancient, bleached timber and hit me painfully on the head. Tom laughed, nodded at the breaker and said, "I'd leave that old bastard alone if I were you, mate. I reckon he's got it in for you."

A letter had arrived from Elena, full of love, there was a lipstick kiss mark on the bottom of the page. Trudy didn't seem quite as cross with me as she had been. She'd been very quiet, but she hadn't thrown any more food at me. My bike was all fuelled up and serviced, it sat in the garage waiting to go. My dad had finished the top box for all my gear—it had a false bottom which could be lifted out with a small space below it where I could stow my valuables. I'd painted it black and stuck a Kenny Roberts sticker on the side and a GB sticker on the back. I couldn't wait to start the journey back to my girl.

On my last night, I broke our golden rule and walked to Tom's house to say goodbye.

Tom, Phil, and Sue were sitting in the kitchen when I walked in. There was no sign of Trudy. Maybe she was at Kim's house. We sat and talked for a while, and Sue opened a bottle of wine to toast my departure, Phil had paid me my wages the day before, and he'd been very generous.

"You take your time, son," he'd said, "and if you want to turn around and come home, remember there's no shame in that."

Sue gave me a big hug and kiss and thrust a foil-wrapped parcel into my hands. "I made you a quiche for the journey, Danny."

"Thanks, Sue," I said, genuinely touched by her kindness and knowing what a challenge cooking could be for her. "I'll think of you when I'm eating it."

I tried to ignore Phil and Tom's mime act, retching with their fingers down their throats, behind Sue's back.

"Where's Trudy?" I asked.

Sue glanced at her husband, "She's gone out, Danny. She's been a bit upset lately. Don't worry. She'll be all right."

Tom and I said goodbye on the doorstep. "See you later, mate," he said. We shook hands and then slightly self-consciously we hugged each other, probably for the first time since we were little. Hugging your best mate wasn't a commonplace thing in the 1970s and feeling slightly embarrassed we both quickly reverted back to our backslapping, piss-taking default setting.

"Go on. Sod off, you homo. Send me a postcard and give her one for me."

"Yeah, see you later, masturbator," I replied.

It was a relief when he scruffed my quiff and pushed me out of the door before either one of us did anything else stupid or emotional.

Trudy was waiting for me under the third lamp post down the lane, she was leaning on the granite stone wall that ran around the park perimeter.

"Hi, Trude, I went to your house to say goodbye."

"Yeah, I know," she replied, "I wanted to speak to you on your own."

She put her arms around my neck and kissed me. I kissed her back and held her for a moment. She felt lovely in my arms.

"Why have you got to go, Danny? You've got everything you need right here. Sorry about the chips," she added, looking slightly contrite. "It was just a bit of a shock when you said you were leaving."

She was sweet and composed. This was the calm before the storm, and I was preparing myself for the worst, but it never came.

"I love her, Trudy," I said quietly, looking her in the eyes.

"Well, stay here and love me instead," she replied, "I'm not a little kid anymore, you know."

She kissed me again, and she turned and walked off without looking back. I think she was hoping I'd follow her, but instead, I watched her until she got to her door, where she turned and looked back once. She'd given it her best shot and caught me completely off guard with her cool, calm routine. It was an Oscar-winning performance, classic Trudy. She really was an extraordinary girl, and for just a moment I asked myself if I was doing the right thing, letting this little gem slip through my fingers. I could stay in the village and start dating her, she was pretty and funny, and I liked being with her. She was everything that most boys could have wished for, but she wasn't Elena. Whenever I thought about the Spanish girl, my guts churned and being without her gave me an empty feeling inside. I was sixteen years old, but I knew she was the only one for me. I walked across the park to my house. There were tears in my eyes.

I woke up to my alarm at 4 am and crept downstairs, put my food into my rucksack and checked for the hundredth time that I'd got everything. Outside it was dry, and the air was full of high summer. There were Pipistrelle bats still on the night shift, hunting insects around the solitary streetlamp at the bottom of our cul-de-sac. I pushed my bike up the street so as not to wake my folks, then kicked it up. With a lump in my throat and a photo of a beautiful Spanish girl in my jacket pocket, I rode out of my childhood village home.

THIRTEEN

The King Is Dead, And The Khazis
Are Okay

I was about nine hours on the road to Dover, forty miles per hour on small roads, my super loud pea shooter exhaust pipe ringing in my ears like a crazy mosquito. I stopped at a greasy spoon just outside of Dover, for a cup of tea. There was a dozen or so bikes parked outside.

In the cafe, 'Rockin Robin' by The Jackson 5 was playing on the jukebox. Seeing my bike in the car park, piled high with gear, one of the bikers shouted, "Bloody hell, mate. Is there a Fizzy under that lot?"

They asked me where I was going.

"Spain," I told them.

They were impressed. One of them remarked, "Bleeding ell, I thought we was doing well riding all the way from The Isle 'O' Dogs."

They were a gang of motorcyclists, boys and girls on a ride out from London. Every weekend, they told me, they left the crowded city behind and blasted down the twisty roads of rural Kent, stopping at cafes and pubs, sometimes heading for Dover, sometimes Margate or Southend. This little place on the outskirts of town was one of their regular haunts.

Me and my mates loved transport cafes. They were a big part of our youth. Even before we had motorbikes, we'd cycle to our local cafe on the A46 to play the pinball machines, eat bacon sandwiches, and listen to records on the jukebox. When we finally became motorized, we'd spend half our lives in cafes. To kids like us, from a village, busy transport cafes were like crossroads that the whole world seemed to pass through. We once saw Steve Gibbons and his band sitting in Greasy Lil's on the A5 near Cannock, eating chip butties at three in the morning. We loved the late-night clientele, musicians coming back from gigs, truck drivers and bikers, the tomato-shaped ketchup dispensers on the Formica tables, and the smell of chips, bacon, and coffee, mixed with the thick fog of cigarette smoke that always hung in the air. Everybody smoked in the sixties and seventies. Even our village doctor sat at the bar of The White Lion, puffing away on roll-ups as he sipped his Pedigree bitter.

The old lady behind the counter with a gold leaf hanging out of the corner of her mouth looked up and said to me, "Allo, deary. Whad'ya want?"

I hardly dared breath as the long pillar of ash on the end of her cigarette hung dangerously over the Mothers Pride she was buttering. Taking my life into my hands, I ordered tea and a chip butty, she said, "Go and sit down, lovely. Sharon'll bring it over."

I went and sat with the bikers at a table by the

window and Sharon, a brassy teenage blonde with nicotine-stained fingers, a tight skirt, and a sassy attitude brought me my food, she winked at me and smiled. "Ain't seen you around here before, 'andsome."

The London kids whooped, laughed, banged the tables. One of the boys called after the waitress, "Didn't take you long, Shal, did it, darling?" Then to me, "Watch her, mate. She'll eat you for breakfast. You'll never get to Spain if dirty Shal gets hold of you first."

The waitress smiled, gave a two-fingered salute, and mouthed "Piss off" at him. It was all good-natured, though.

The youths asked me about my journey, and I told them my story. I showed them the photo of the Spanish girl that I kept in my pocket, which elicited the usual wolf whistles, raised eyebrows, and ever-so-slightly smutty remarks from the lads. One of the girls sitting opposite me, with her elbows on the table and her chin cupped in her hand, was staring at me dreamily as she simultaneously ate chips and smoked a cigarette. "Ahh, you ain't half romantic, ain'tcha?"

I got to the ticket office around 2:30 PM and bought a one-way ticket for a ferry which was sailing early evening into Calais. By now I had continuous butterflies in my stomach. I couldn't believe that I was on my way back to my girl. I followed the rest of the traffic up the loading ramp and boarded the boat. It was high season, and the ferry was rammed full, most of the passengers were in cars pulling caravans or piled high with luggage. My bike was tied to rails in the vehicle deck alongside a dozen other bikes, mostly big Japanese tourers laden with camping gear. I got a coffee and leant on the deck rails at the back of the boat, watching the great propellers churning up the oily portside water as we left the harbour.

It wasn't until I saw the white cliffs disappearing into the distance that I suddenly realised the enormity of what I was doing. For a few brief minutes, I felt a little bit sick, not from the motion of the boat but because I could see the English coastline growing ever more distant and taking me away from everything and everybody who was familiar to me. It didn't last for long though, because later when I walked to the other end of the boat and looked at the coast of France looming on the horizon, I felt instantly better because I knew that that was the direction back to my girlfriend.

I rode off the ramp and into France, riding on the wrong side of the road for the first time. It was a bit strange at first, but I just followed the bikes in front. Most of the traffic was heading the same way as me—holidaymakers, caravans, cars and buses heading to Brittany and the south. I planned to ride to Orleans first, about 270 miles down the road, then ride south-east towards Limoges. I wanted to cross the mountains at Andorra or farther east, near Perpignan, depending on how the little bike performed on the gradients with all the weight on board.

I headed down the route national following the signs for Rouen and rode for an hour or so, until it started to get dark, when I pulled off the main road and pitched my tent in a thicket of trees next to a country lane. I checked my speedo. I'd ridden nearly 200 miles in the last sixteen hours. I lit my stove, had a cup of tea, then slept like a baby for twelve hours.

In the morning, I woke up with that 'where the bloody hell am I?' feeling. I got out of my tent to a beautiful day with birds singing under expansive blue skies.

I stretched and took a great lungful of fresh French country air, I had a coughing fit, and lit a smoke. Just because I was in a foreign country, there was no reason to compromise my usual morning routine. I had enough water left to make a brew then I checked the bike over, packed my gear, and hit the road.

When I reached Boulogne, I called at a filling station for petrol. I bought postcards and stamps, and in a Boulangerie I bought some bread and *'pain au chocolat,'* an incredible buttery pastry oozing with chocolate which could have been designed for a teenager's breakfast. I sat in the morning sunshine and wrote cards to my family and Trudy and Tom.

"Arrived safely in France. Bike's running well. Two hundred miles yesterday. Going steadier today. Had cake for breakfast. Nearly ran out of proper smokes. Gonna have to buy some French ones soon, even though they're horrible. Missing you all. Love, Danny."

I could imagine my mam's excitement when she got the card in a few days. Then, with a slight pang of guilt, I remembered that she was probably expecting me to come home, with my tail between my legs in the next twenty-four hours.

From Boulogne to Abbeville, I rode through rolling green countryside, which reminded me of England. Plump, buttery cows, Jerseys, Friesians, and Charolais, grazing in sunny green pastures looked up nonchalantly at the noisy English boy passing by on his screamingly loud moped. I made good time heading towards Rouen and ten miles or so from the city I stopped for the night at a municipal campsite in a pretty village. There were showers and 'proper' toilets. I'd first encountered the French 'hole in the ground' type toilets on my school trip to Boulogne, and it'd been a bit of a culture shock. The campsite toilets, though, were just the same as the ones back home except there were no toilet seats. I thought it was a bit strange that they couldn't go the extra mile and bung a seat on the porcelain. Perhaps there was a national shortage of bog seats, or the French were going through a bathroom evolution, slowly introducing the population to proper toilets.

I tended to overthink things sometimes, and I blamed my grandad for my toilet critiquing habit. He liked a nice, clean convenience. Whenever he went on a day trip with the old folks in the village, he'd always give us a full report on the state of the toilets, or 'Khazis', as the old Eastender called them.

"How was the miniature village in Bourton On the Water, grandad?" I once asked him after a bus trip with the Methodist chapel old-timers.

"It was pretty average, son," he replied, "but the khazi's was bloody lovely. Clean as a whistle and nice, soft paper."

My Grandad didn't half make me laugh. I was going to miss him.

I'd bought some sausages from the butchers in the village and a bottle of wine at the store, which was cheaper than petrol, though only slightly better tasting. The campsite attendant came to collect the fee and charged me two and a half francs (around thirty pence). A few more campers turned up later—a couple of families, probably heading south, and a group of cyclists. Camping in France was brilliant, French campsites seemed to be excellent and cheap as well. I lay on the grass outside my tent as the sun went down. Rocksteady playing on the cassette player. I wondered what Tom and Trudy were doing. I was missing them. Once again, I felt a pang of longing for my home, and especially for my two best friends. I'd write to them both soon. Meantime, I was desperate to speak to Elena and let her know that I was on my way.

Next morning, back on the route National, I flashed through small villages and towns, pretty and pastoral with red tile or slate-roofed cottages, cafes, *Les Routier's* truck stops, and bars lined the highway. Later on after Rouen, the land became flatter, and pasture and woodland were replaced by huge prairie fields of golden corn and maize. The sun was beating down mercilessly, and even after I'd bungeed my leather jacket to my top box and rode in a T-shirt, it was still unbearable. The hot air in my face was like being blasted with a hairdryer. The sun reflected the heat from the cornfields and then threw it right back at me until I felt like an ant under a magnifying glass. It was like riding through a furnace. The tar had started to melt on the roads, leaving sticky patches of black pitch exposed by the wheels of the traffic. The little bike didn't like the heat too much either, and I had to stop several times to clean the carbon deposits from my spark plug and let her cool down. She would have probably seized from the heat otherwise.

Approaching the city of Chartres, I saw the tall twin gothic spires of the cathedral rising majestically from the flat land, shimmering in a heat haze from the fierce afternoon sun. The vast agricultural landscape was strange and foreign to my eyes. Dumpy squat pylons, side by side, two by two, marched over the cornfields, glass insulators shining like strings of diamonds, concrete, post-modern, sci-fi water towers peeped over the occasional thickets of trees like 'B movie' flying saucers about to invade.

Finally, the landscape became a little more forgiving. The sun started to lose its power, and long, shady boulevards of trees lined the roads. My head was thumping, and I was dehydrated.

I felt battered by the heat and the lack of food and water. By Early evening I was about ten miles north of Orleans. I stopped in a medium-sized village. There were signs in the square for a municipal campsite. It had cooled down, and the blazing heat of the day had transformed into a beautiful, fragrant evening. I pulled up by the 'Friterie,' a converted Citroen van with a serving hatch in its side, the smell of chips frying made me realise how hungry I was. There were half a dozen kids about my age sitting on a wall under some trees beside the chip van, and there were a few motorbikes parked on the road in front of them, some modern sports bikes, mopeds and a Velosolex—the eccentric little front-wheel-drive cycle motor used by everybody in France, from the midwife to the village paperboy. The whole scene reminded me of 'the cross' back home. There was even a cafe bar across the street.

At the chip van I asked for '*frites grande et limonade s'il vous plaît*,' the man served the chips in a large upside-down cone made from rolled-up paper, with a dollop of mayonnaise slapped on the top, I was starving, and they were amazing. As I was wolfing them down, two boys and a girl got up from the wall and walked over to look at my bike.

One of the boys nodded at me. "*Bonsoir*."

I nodded back at them. "*Bonsoir*."

"*Anglais?*" asked the boy, pointing at the GB sticker on my top box.

They were curious to find out what an English youth was doing in rural France on a moped, so again, I started telling my story—this time in pidgin French with some English thrown in. Pascal, one of the boys, knew a little bit of English, and his girlfriend, Sylvie, spoke English quite well. We muddled through, and with some help translating from Sylvie, they learned about my crazy moped pilgrimage to Spain. They invited me to the bar across the street, but I told them I had to get to the campsite before it closed for the evening. I said I'd see them there later.

The campsite was in a pretty spot on the edge of the village by the river. I pitched my tent, had a shower, and walked the half-mile back to the square. I called Elena from the public phone box near the bar and told her where I was. The payphone was devouring my francs, so we spoke only for a few minutes. It was wonderful to hear her voice. She was amazed how far I'd travelled since we'd last talked in England. She said that her mam had spoken to her aunt in Lloret De Mar, and good old Pili had given me a glowing report.

Elena had taken a leap of faith and told her mam that I was on my way to Albarracin so we could be together. She said her mam thought we were crazy, but she was on our side. They hadn't plucked up the courage to tell her dad yet. Elena asked how my parents had felt about my leaving England, and I told her that my folks didn't think I'd get any farther than Dover. She felt sorry for my mam and she told me I should call her and tell her I was okay. She was right. I should, but I was still feeling a bit smug about proving my parents wrong, so I thought I'd let them stew a bit longer first.

We were both happy and excited. It seemed that if I could keep this pace up, we'd be together again in maybe a week and a half.

We said goodbye. I imagined her standing there behind the counter in the campsite reception, my girl, beautiful, warm, funny, and only a thousand miles of black tarmac between us. I missed her so much it hurt.

The bar was busy, and more kids had joined the earlier crowd, Pascal handed me a bottle of cold beer. He was quite formal when he introduced me to the others. The boys shook my hand, and the girls kissed me on the cheek. Some of the boys even kissed each other. God knows what Tom would have said. I smiled at the thought. They were very civilised, friendly, and hospitable—a common trait of the *bloody horrible Normans*

I was discovering—and they were good company. We drank beer, played billiards and table football. They called it 'baby-foot,' and they played it with conviction, spinning the spindles with amazing speed and skill.

There was a jukebox in the corner, but I didn't recognise many of the songs. There was no ska, reggae, or punk rock. Pascal put in a coin and invited me to pick a record, so I chose a France Gall song, "Laisse Tomber Les Filles," from the 1960s. Sylvie laughed and said it was an old-fashioned song that her parents listened to. I told her that I'd loved France Gall ever since I'd seen her win the Eurovision Song Contest on our black and white telly when I was 5 years old.

Everything was comfortingly familiar in the bar, the cigarette smoke, the laughter, the smell of chips wafting in from the friterie outside. I wondered who was at 'The Cross 'tonight, and if my mam and dad were in 'The Lion' laughing and drinking with the Greens. Once again I felt the familiar little lurch in my stomach as I thought about home. Later, I said goodbye to the French kids in the bar and with calls of bon voyage and bonne chance ringing in my ears, I walked back to the camp-site. I needed to get a good night's sleep and start getting those miles behind me.

I headed out early the next morning, stopping at the boulangerie in the village for *pain au chocolat* to eat on the road. Left to my own devices, I seemed to be settling into a steady diet of cake, chips, sausages, bread, and beer—the 1970s teenage equivalent of 'five a day,' or six if you include cigarettes. I went into the Tabac shop next door and bought a packet of Gauloises. Glancing at the newspapers on my way out I noticed the headline on the front of every paper: 'ELVIS PRESLEY *EST MORT.*' I picked up a tacky tabloid journal from the stand, and with my limited French, I read that he'd died in Graceland on his golden toilet the previous day from a heart attack. At least he'd probably had a comfortable seat. My grandad would have approved. I'd never really been a big fan, but I knew my mam would be sad. 'Elv the Pelv' was her teenage heartthrob.

That day I rode one hundred and thirty miles and stopped in a village twenty miles or so from Limoges. It was a tough ride. It had rained steadily all day, and I got pretty damp despite stopping to put my waterproofs on.

I found a callbox and called my mam. It was funny to think of her all those miles away, standing at the bottom of our stairs, speaking into the trimphone. She sounded pleased to hear from me, though.

"You all right, love? Where are you?"

"I'm fine, Mam. I'm in Limoges."

"Limoges! Where's that?"

"It's about a third of the way down France, Mam."

"What are you doing a third of the way down France? For goodness' sakes, Daniel, don't you think you should come back home now?" She was bordering on mild hysteria and starting to sound like the 'Spam' lady from 'Monty Python's Flying Circus.'

"I'm on my way to Spain, Mam, like I told you and Dad last week."

I heard my dad in the background, saying, "Where is the silly bugger, Sal?"

. . .

"You're being ridiculous and stubborn, Daniel, just like your bloody father. You can't go gallivanting off to Spain just for some silly girl that you met on holiday." And then to my dad: "I blame you for this, Frankie Wilbur."

"She's not a silly girl, Mam. She's amazing. Wait till you meet her. It's serious. She's the girl I'm going to be with, and you'll have to get used to the idea."

"Listen, Daniel," she remonstrated, "come home now and think about it for a little while, love. If you still feel the same way, then you can go back out to this girl of yours next spring. Me and your dad'll help you," she said, then added, "Remember that girl in the Chemists? You thought she was the 'one and only', didn't you? I'm still finding plastic combs and toothbrushes all over the house. Your dad found one down the back of the sofa last night when he was looking for his fag lighter."

I made my excuses. "Mam, I've got to go. This call's costing me a fortune. I'll ring you later, and don't worry about me."

I put the phone back in its cradle before she could start asking me if I was eating properly and washing behind my ears. Well, at least I'd called her as I promised Elena I would, and at least she knew I was okay. If she could have looked into my future for the next few weeks though, she'd have 'had kittens', to coin one of her favourite phrases.

The sun came out as I pitched my tent in a busy little campsite on the outskirts of the village close to a small lake with a beach. I hung my damp clothes on a tree to dry, put my favourite tape on the cassette player, and cooked some sausages on my camp stove. The weather was beautiful now. The rain had stopped, the sky was blue, and my clothes were steaming in the last rays of the evening sun. After dinner, I sat under a tree, drank a bottle of beer, closed my eyes, and thought about the Spanish girl.

FOURTEEN

Johnny Too Bad

THE FOLLOWING day was fine and hot. I travelled around 120 miles even though I had to stop several times to clean the spark plug, and once to bolt the expansion chamber back on when it dropped off. The ride was nice though, the long straight, sun-dappled roads through endless forests suited me better than the baking hot sun and open landscapes of the Loire.

Early evening, I stopped at a campsite in a heavily forested area on the site of a shrine dedicated to a young shepherdess. According to the information board which was written in three languages, the tragic young woman was killed by wolves while tending her flock centuries ago. A whole legend had grown up around this place. Visions had been seen, diseases cured, and the lame had walked. It was a bit like a pound shop Lourdes. It all looked a bit touristy with a bar-restaurant on the edge of a car park large enough to accommodate the busloads of French nuns and pilgrims who probably visited during the season.

A hundred and fifty yards behind the campsite on a rocky outcrop, there was a vast, twenty-foot-high concrete statue of the unfortunate girl and a slightly garish grotto. I checked the camping rates displayed near to the reception. It was quite expensive to pitch a tent, but I hadn't seen anywhere else nearby to camp, and the bar looked inviting. The smell of food cooking was making my poor empty belly rumble, so I decided to stay for the food and then try and fly-pitch my tent after dark to save a few francs.

On the edge of the car park, at the side of the bar, was a mown grass field probably used for overspill parking. I could pitch the tent there later and sneak into the site to use the washrooms at first light. I could hear Tom's voice in my head telling me not to be such a 'tight git.'

I parked my bike outside of the bar and went in for a well-earned beer and some food. Inside it was decorated in a faux-medieval style, with ancient rustic tools and weapons hanging on the whitewashed walls. It was tacky, but I liked tacky. The place was busy, there were lots of hikers and campers, including a party of noisy young German kids about my age. They were on holiday, I supposed, eating, laughing, and drinking, they looked like they were enjoying themselves. Old French pop songs were playing through the bar room speakers, and some of the Germans were singing along to the 'Ye-Ye Girl 'songs.

The menu was cheap and cheerful. I ordered pizza from the wood-burning oven and cold beer. I sat down at the only empty table, next to the German kids, who all seemed friendly. They raised their glasses and said' Prost and Santé'. The barman was friendly too, and so were the girls who were serving the food. They were dressed in medieval serving wench costumes, long skirts with tight bodices and white blouses, like 'extras' from a *Hammer House of Horror Dracula* movie set. It was all for the benefit of the tourists, I supposed. Either that or I'd accidentally slipped into one of those urban legend French time warps that I'd read about in my dad's Sunday *Titbits* magazine.

The English couple, desperate for somewhere to stay one dark night, stop their car at a pretty Chambre d 'hote in the middle of the remote French countryside. The old French couple who run the rustic little place are charmingly old-fashioned and serve the tourists a delicious meal on earthenware plates by candlelight. The hotel has no electricity, TV, or radio, and the couple retires to their clean and tidy whitewashed bedroom by candlelight. They're charmed by the romance and simplicity of the place and vow to call again on their way back upcountry. But returning a week later, they find the building has disappeared into thin air. They quiz the locals, only to be told that there hasn't been a hotel in that area for nearly one hundred years.

My dad debunked the myth in seconds: "France is a big country. One old hotel looks pretty well like another. There was no electricity because there was a power cut that night, and the silly buggers never found the place again because his missus was probably reading the map upside-down."

The atmosphere in the bar was nice. It was still warm outside, the doors were open, and the ceiling fans were whirring overhead. Camper's children were playing on swings and slides in a play area in front of the bar while their parents sat at tables on the terrace. When my food came, it was good. There was a French bar billiard table at one end of the room, and two men were playing while a girl looked on. The men were short, thick set, each with a cigarette in the corner of their mouths, blinking the smoke from their eyes as they concentrated on their shots. They looked like brothers or close relatives. The girl was small too, quite pretty with long, suicide blonde hair, dressed in tight flared jeans, platform shoes and a cheesecloth shirt. She was about my age, I guessed, maybe sixteen or seventeen years old. I noticed she was looking my way quite a lot and smiling. After I'd finished eating, she approached me and said something, but she spoke quite fast, and with my 'O' level French, I couldn't understand her too well, so I just smiled and said, "*Bonsoir.*" When I went to the bar for another drink, the barmen raised an eyebrow at me, nodded towards the group of three at the billiard table, and pointed at his eye—international language for "Watch out. They're bad news."

I got up to leave at around ten o'clock. The Germans invited me to stay for another drink. They were a friendly crowd, and like most young Germans, they all seemed to speak English well. They were good company, and I was tempted to stay, but I'd had a long day. After a couple of beers and with a full belly, I was ready to sleep.

The girl caught my eye, gave me a little wave, and smiled again as I left, but I just nodded at the three of them. The men were still playing billiards, but I noticed they looked up as I left the bar.

Outside, it was dark now, I could fly pitch the tent in the field without much chance of being seen. I rode down the driveway before turning off my lights and veering off-road. I pitched the tent next to the bike, rolled out my sleeping bag, and lay on top of it. I could still see the distant lights from the restaurant through the canvas. The night was warm and, and there was a sky full of stars. I closed my eyes and thought about my girl-friend lying in her bed in a town somewhere in the middle of Spain that I'd never seen. I wondered what Tom and Trudy were doing back at home. I'd be at the halfway point in my journey soon. Spain was getting closer, as my old life in England was getting farther away. I was fast asleep in a few minutes.

I awoke with a start to a noise outside. Somebody was speaking, a girl's voice, hushed but urgent, saying, "*Monsieur, Monsieur*," and shaking the canvas door of the tent.

I looked at my watch. It was 1:30 am. I sat up and quickly pulled on my T-shirt and jeans and undid the tent flap from the inside.

It was the blonde girl from the bar, she started to crawl into the tent. Remembering the barman's warn-ing, I pushed her out by her shoulders, shouting, "Get the fuck out!" I followed her into the field where she fired a ripe volley of French curses at me, before making an unmistakable gesture with her middle finger and stomping off into the darkness.

I was wide awake, and I didn't want to go back to

sleep now. I expected trouble, maybe the two men she'd been with would come back and try to rob me. I sat in the tent doorway for around an hour, straining my eyes and ears at the inky darkness, but there was nothing to be seen or heard, so I hoped that she'd gone for good. Tiredness eventually got the better of me, so I crawled back into my sleeping bag, and although I tried to stay awake, I soon fell back into a deep exhausted sleep.

I woke early, around 6:30 am, and slipped out of my tent, still dressed from the disturbance in the night. I wanted to creep in and use the washrooms before too many campers woke up.

As I walked towards the campsite, I glanced back over my shoulder at the tent, and something looked wrong. At first, I couldn't see what it was, and then it hit me. My bike wasn't there. I ran back and stupidly walked around the tent, half expecting to find it there, but it was gone. I guessed it was those bastards from the bar. The girl had probably intended to steal the keys when she tried to get into my tent. I should have stayed awake after she'd gone, or even better, moved my bike and tent onto the campsite and paid the bill in the morning.

I was in a blind panic. I ran down to the woodland track that bordered the field and looked around for half an hour in the vain hope that they'd got fed up with pushing it and had dumped it nearby. I walked back to the tent, packed everything into my rucksack, and headed towards the bar. The barman from the previous evening wasn't there, though the bar was open for coffee and for campers to collect their bread, delivered every morning from the village bakery. I tried to explain to the girl behind the bar what had happened, but she didn't speak much English. I was panicking, and every time I tried to speak French, it came out mixed up with the Spanish that I'd been learning from my phrasebook.

Thankfully one of the German boys from the group in the bar the night before came in to buy bread, and he translated my panicky, garbled nonsense to the girl. She immediately picked up the phone and phoned the village *gendarmerie*, the young German bought me a coffee and sat and waited with me. I was in a bit of a state. I told him all about Elena and how desperate I was to get to Spain. I explained to him that nearly everything that I owned was locked in the top box on the bike, including most of the money that I needed for my journey. He was a nice guy. He said, "don't worry," he and his friends would help me if they could.

The village *gendarme* turned up surprisingly quickly. He was a young man, quite grave and formal. Via my new German friend, I gave him all the details of my stolen bike. He asked us for descriptions of the men and the girl in the bar and asked me to explain exactly what had happened during the night. After sharpening his pencil with a penknife, he carefully and pedantically wrote everything down in his little pocketbook, before telling me to stay at the campsite while he went to scout out the locality to see if there was any sign of my bike.

I walked back with my new friend, Jan, to the family-sized tent and VW camper van he was sharing with some of the people in his party. They gave me some breakfast and more coffee, though I didn't feel much like eating, and Jan recounted my predicament to his friends. After an anxious two and a half hour wait, the *gendarme* pulled up in his car and announced he'd found my bike. Someone had reported it dumped in a farm gateway a mile or so out of the nearby village.

Jan and I jumped into the *gendarme*'s car, and he took us to retrieve it. It was leaning up against a hedge, the padlock smashed off the top box, the steering lock broken, and the wires on the back of the ignition switch had been cut to hotwire the bike and start it. Most of my clothes were strewn on the grass. Everything seemed to be there except for my Levi's jeans and jacket, and my tool bag. Then my heart sank as I noticed the plywood board, which made the false bottom of my top box, had been pulled out and thrown into the hedge. I'd left my money under this board. My stomach lurched, and I felt sick. Now I had a big problem.

The *gendarme* said that he was pretty sure the people in the bar had taken the bike. He didn't know much about them except the barmaid had told him that the older of the two men was called Jean-Marie, Johnny to his friends. She said she didn't like him very much. There was around £50 in sterling and francs taken from my top box. The policeman said he'd check the local banks in case anybody had tried to change pounds for francs that morning, but he didn't seem too optimistic. I'd got the bike, though, and I was grateful for that. I thanked him sincerely for his help, picked up my few remaining possessions, twisted the ignition wires together, started the bike, and followed the police car back to the campsite. I had about fifty French francs in my wallet, which was about five pounds sterling. I was in the middle of a foreign country, and I didn't even have a decent pair of jeans. I had some serious thinking to do.

My bike was my only asset, but if I had no other option, then I'd sell it. One thing I was sure about, though, I'd get to Elena somehow, even if I had to walk to Spain. Jan took me back to his tent, and I sat with him and his friends, I put a brave face on, but I was feeling a bit sorry for myself. One of the boys went to the bar and came back with some beer. I repeated my story to the rest of the group, everything from meeting Elena in Lloret De Mar, to being robbed the night before. I showed them some pictures of my girlfriend, which thankfully hadn't been stolen from my top box. They were nice kids and sympathetic. I was thankful that Jan had been in the bar to help me that morning. The German girls, who thought it was all incredibly romantic, told me they'd been grape picking the summer before. They said it would be a great way to get enough cash together to finish my trip. They told me Languedoc was an area where the '*Verdange*'or grape harvest usually started quite early in the season, and they were always desperate for workers in the vine-yards. If I headed to this region, then I wouldn't be going too far out of my way, and I could cross the mountains at Andorra or Perpignan. One of the girls fetched her diary out of the tent and leafed through the pages until she found an address and phone number. She wrote it down on a scrap of paper and handed it to me.

"Try this place, we were there last year. They're

friendly people, and the camping ground on the farm is very good, with showers."

Jan fetched a map from the VW and spread it on the grass.

"Look, Danny, if you go across the country on the small roads, it should be no more than four hundred kilometres. You could make it in maybe two days."

Suddenly everything seemed possible again, and I started to feel a lot better.

God, I loved these Germans! They were just so bloody practical.

If I was careful with my remaining cash, I should be able to make it to the vineyards and my first payday by the skin of my teeth if I didn't eat much and didn't buy cigarettes and beer. The German kids cooked an enormous dinner that evening, we stayed up late and drank beer around the campfire. They gave my battered morale a big boost. Before we turned in for the night, we exchanged addresses and promised to keep in touch.

The next day I was up early, packing my gear and preparing to leave. I crept around trying not to wake my friends, but Jan heard me and pretty soon most of them were up, bleary-eyed, and slightly hungover, to wave me goodbye. With everything loaded and tied on the bike, I shook hands with them all and thanked them one more time. Jan handed me a brown paper bag. I looked inside. There was a small roll of paper money.

"Danny, I hope you won't be offended, but we passed the hat around for you."

I didn't know what to say. I made a feeble attempt at refusing the money, for the sake of polite convention.

I tried to thank them, but I really couldn't find the words to express how grateful I was. If they hadn't been there to help me, I would have been in a desperate situation. I hoped we'd meet again sometime so I could repay them all. Feeling slightly emotional, I kicked up the bike, and rode off down the dusty track, waving at my new friends. In the space of twenty-four hours, I'd met the very worst and the very best kinds of people.

France is a big country, but karma is amazing.

Nearly eight hours later, heading south-west on the route national I rode past a garage, and leaning against the tailboard of a battered pick-up truck, I spotted a familiar figure. Bleached blonde hair, like a flag, she was looking bored and smoking a cigarette, while her companion chatted to the petrol pump attendant. The most striking thing about the girl were her clothes: a faded Levi's jacket with a distinctive Trojan records badge sewed onto the right arm, and a 'Keep the Faith' patch on the left. It was Johnny the bastard and the teenage honey trap.

I nearly fell off my bike in amazement, but she hardly gave me a second glance as I rode by. Heart thumping, I pulled over a hundred yards up the road, pushed my bike into a field gateway and parked behind a hedge. I thought about finding a call box and phoning the *gendarmes*, but I knew it would be a waste of time. Even if I could explain myself in pidgin French to a copper, the pair would be miles away by the time the law turned up.

When they drove off up the road a few minutes later, I followed them, keeping a discreet distance behind the truck, which was piled high with scrap metal. They turned off the main road after a few miles and rattled down a country lane, before driving down a dirt track towards a dilapidated single-story house amidst run-down sheds and outbuildings. Concealed by a hedge, I watched them from the end of the drive. They parked the truck by a cowshed a hundred yards or so from the house, and Johnny started to unload the scrap from the back, throwing it into piles of various types of metal. The girl walked to the house and unlocked the front door. Several large dogs of dubious pedigrees came bounding out to greet her.

I slipped off, as quietly as I could and rode a few miles down the road. In a nearby village, I sat on the bank of a river and waited. The sun was beating down, and I took the opportunity to doze in the shade for a couple of hours. I needed some rest because I was going to be busy that night.

Later, I walked over the street to the village store and spent some of my scant funds on a one-kilo bag of sugar. I waited until around 11:30 PM before making my way back to the shanty. The lights stayed on in the house until around 1 AM. I waited another hour after the last light went out before creeping down the dark junk-lined driveway.

As quietly as I possibly could I started to systemati-cally trash the truck. I pulled the petrol filler cap off and poured the bag of sugar into the tank along with several large handfuls of the dry sandy soil under my feet. I punctured the sidewall of each tyre with the sharp end of my lock knife and waited for ten minutes or so until the hissing of air had stopped, before making a five-inch slash in each one, rendering them unrepairable.

I turned the big chrome handle on the front of the truck and lifted the bonnet. The hinges screeched alarmingly. I held my breath for a minute or so, listening for any noise from the house, but thankfully, silence prevailed. I unscrewed the oil filler cap and scooped in more sandy soil and several handfuls of small pebbles into the engine before slowly and quietly closing the bonnet. Then, just for good measure, I picked up a bar of iron from the scrap pile and pushed it into the radiator, twisting and turning it until the water was running out like a colander.

Happy with my work, I crept off, sticking to the shadows, thankful that the dogs hadn't woken up. I pushed my bike quite a way down the lane before starting it and heading back to the village.

There was no camping place, but the night was warm, so I rolled out my sleeping bag and slept by the river, under the stars. It took me ages to get to sleep. I was excited and really pleased with myself. I wished Tom was with me, he'd have loved this.

I woke around eight am, packed my kit and rode back to the scene of the crime. I was looking forward to seeing the aftermath of my nightshift. I cut the engine and coasted the last hundred yards. From the top of the dirt driveway, I could hear raised voices. Johnny was walking around his truck, kicking the tyres and cursing, while the girl was sitting glumly on a pile of old roof tiles with her head in her hands. She was still wearing my jacket.

The best would come later, though. Hopefully, Johnny would spend a small fortune on replacing the tyres. He'd fit them, and then he'd try to start his truck. The sugar and grit in his fuel tank and sump would soon wreck the engine and stop it dead. His problems would be compounded by the radiator which would leak water like a sieve. The truck was a complete write-off. Stealing my gear had cost them dearly.

I kicked up the bike. Johnny and his daughter looked up at the sudden noise. I rode into full view at the top of their drive, revved my engine, and gave them the old two-fingered Saxon salute. It was a great moment. Tom and Trudy would have been proud of me. I felt like Zorro as I rode up the lane.

FIFTEEN

Pressure Drop

RIDING SOUTH, the landscape was becoming wilder and hillier with thick woodland either side of the road. The last village I'd passed through was almost twenty miles ago. I'd considered stopping there and looking for a place to spend the night, but the early evening had seemed fine and dry, so I carried on. Now though, the sky had begun to get very dark, and even though I was buzzing along at forty mph, the humidity had become almost unbearable. There was the fizz of electricity in the air and a faint smell of ozone and rain. It looked like I was heading right into a storm of biblical proportions. The occasional cars heading from the direction I was travelling towards, had their headlights on full—always a bad sign. I started looking for a place to stop, and shelter before the deluge inevitably began, a bridge or a barn. Anywhere would do. I just needed to stay dry and wait out the storm because if I got a soaking, then I'd be wet and uncomfortable all night.

I spotted a stone building fifty yards or so from the

road, nestled in a hollow on the edge of woodland. I pulled up to investigate. There was a gateway with a rotten old five bar gate across it and a rutted cart track that was overgrown and looked like it hadn't been used for years. I pushed open the gate and walked up the track just as the first fat, warm raindrops began to fall. It was an ancient two-story farm building with an open cowshed attached to the side. It looked almost medieval in design. A stone staircase on the outside of the house accessed the upper floor. The roof looked good enough to keep me dry, and most importantly, the place seemed unoccupied.

In seconds, the heavens opened, and the rain started to fall, not in drops now, but in sheets. I ran back down the track, jumped on the bike, and rode towards the building, anxious to get under cover before me, and my kit got soaked. I parked under the shelter of the open-fronted cowshed. The building looked to be a simple stone farmhouse of sorts with a single large room down-stairs and probably the same upstairs. Running through the downpour from the cowshed to the half-open front door, I stepped over the threshold and into a large, gloomy room.

At the back of the house was an ancient inglenook fireplace and in the centre was a 1950s Formica topped kitchen table with a pair of battered old chairs. In the corner a pile of old tins, paint and animal feed, oil cans, and rotting galvanised buckets and tubs. It looked like nobody had lived there for years, though the room was dry, and the fireplace looked usable. There's no doubt, it did look a bit creepy, but with a fire lit for cooking my food, and some music playing on my cassette player, it'd soon be cosy and it was a better prospect than riding through a storm.

I ran back out to the cowshed with my leather jacket over my head and found plenty of dry timber there, which I carried back via a small connecting door between the outbuilding and the kitchen. I unpacked my sleeping kit and rucksack and made camp for the night. I swept the floor with an old hazel broom I found and laid my groundsheet down on the ancient stones. Outside, the storm was raging, and the rain was hammering the pantile roof, water was cascading past the front door, which was wedged, half-open, the wood swollen tight onto the old flagstone floor. Thunder was shaking the old house to its foundations, and fearsome flashes of jagged lightning were illuminating the countryside every thirty seconds or so. It was cooler now. The rain had lowered the temperature, and the sticky humidity had gone. I thought a fire in the grate would cheer things up a bit.

The fire took a little bit of encouragement to start, and I had to drain some petrol out of the bike to pour over the wood, but I soon had an excellent cheery little blaze burning in the hearth. I pressed 'play' on my cassette player, and The Paragons instantly lifted my spirits with "Wear You To The Ball," a song that immediately made me think of Elena. But then, every song seemed to remind me of her. I lit a smoke and put my kettle on the edge of the fire to heat some water for tea. I looked around my temporary accommodation and listened to the rain hammering down outside. I'd had a lucky find with this old place, I thought.

While it was still light, I braved the rain and ran outside with my jacket over my head, to have a look upstairs and double-check that the place was completely unoccupied. The upstairs room was empty with just a pile of old sacks in one corner and some old glass preserving jars stacked against the wall. The roof above me was keeping out the elements, despite the rain still belting down in torrents. I grabbed an armful of the old sacks and shook the dust out of them; they'd be fine under my groundsheet to keep my bones off the hard stone floor.

Around dusk, the rain finally abated. I fried some eggs, ate them with bread and tea, and dozed in front of the fire. I was suddenly shaken out of my sleepy reverie by a knock on the half-open door. A man stood on the doorstep wearing a green waterproof cape, with a rifle case over his shoulder and a pair of pheasants hanging from his belt. He must have seen the bike in the cowshed or noticed the smoke from the chimney when he was passing

"*Bonjour, monsieur,*" I said.

"*Bonsoir, monsieur,*" he replied, correcting me.

"*Ca va je suis ici?*" I asked him if I was okay staying in the place.

He shrugged and told me it wasn't a problem for him. I breathed a sigh of relief. "*Bonne chasse?*" I asked him, trying to make conversation with my limited French and nodding at the pheasants.

"*Ca va*," he replied taciturnly, shrugging again. This fellow wasn't exactly chatty.

"*Monsieur, où est un village?*" I asked.

"*Deux kilomètres,*" he replied, pointing to the road and indicating the direction I'd been travelling before the rain had stopped me.

He mentioned a *chambre d'hotes*. There was accommodation in the village.

I replied, "*Merci, monsieur. Je vais bien,*" though he'd probably already guessed a road battered, English tramp on a moped couldn't afford bed and breakfast.

He looked past me at the room, and I moved out of the way so he could see inside. He peered in and seemed to shiver a little bit. I thought he was probably feeling the cold now that the sun was going down.

He turned on his heel and said, "*Allez, bonne nuit, monsieur, bonne chance.*"

I stood in the doorway and watched as he walked off towards the road. Before he reached the gate, he looked back and shouted again that there was a *chambre d'hote* in the village. He was probably trying to drum up some trade for a relative with a guesthouse.

I poured the last of the tea into my tin mug and sat by the fireside. It was getting dark now, and the rain had cooled the air down nicely. I threw some more wood onto the fire before settling down and falling into a deep, much-needed sleep.

Something woke me later. I don't know what it was, but I woke up with a start. I strained my ears to the sounds of the still night outside. The rain had stopped completely, and apart from the occasional arrhythmical drip, drip of water on vegetation, the night was silent. Just on the edge of my perception, I imagined I could hear a voice or voices, like the distant tinny sound of a radio playing. Then suddenly there was a loud "bump" from the floor above. I froze, petrified.

I reached for my torch and started pulling on my clothes in a panic. There was somebody upstairs, I was sure of it. Seconds later, I heard a dragging sound as if something were being pulled over the old floorboards. Then the unmistakable sound of faint footsteps, running across the floor, quite light, a child's maybe. My mind raced, it could be kids, or someone just dossing down for the night like I was. I looked at my watch; it was 4:50 AM. It would soon be starting to get light outside.

I opened the connecting door to the cowshed and checked on the bike. It was still there, thank God.

Though I was shaking with fear, I tried to be rational. It could be an animal scampering about upstairs. I was pretty sure there was somebody up there, though, and I was expecting trouble. It could even be Johnny the Bastard looking for revenge.

I crept around the outside of the building to the foot of the stone steps. It was dark upstairs with no light showing from the room, and I shone my torch beam up the stairs at the half-open door. Nothing, no sign of life. I relaxed a little bit, but I was still petrified.

It must have been an animal, I told myself.

Though every ounce of good sense I possessed was telling me to get the hell out of this place, I needed to look upstairs and satisfy myself that there was a rational explanation.

I called out, "bonjour, who's there?" There was no answer of course, no talking badgers here I told myself, "this is France, not Narnia." Feeling slightly braver, I crept up the stairs, treading as lightly as possible on the worn, still damp stone steps. Reaching the top, I took a deep breath and nervously shone my torch through the door.

Nothing, the room was empty, I breathed a sigh of relief, "it must have been an animal," I told myself. And the voices I'd heard earlier were probably a farm labourer heading off to work early, listening to a little transistor radio as he passed by on the lane. Then, suddenly a loud "crash" from downstairs like a dozen tin cans being thrown to the floor. Shit! They'd lured me upstairs, and now they were downstairs, probably robbing my gear. My heart thumping, I ran down the stone steps, adrenaline coursing through my veins, I was ready to fight for my life. I wished to god that Tom was with me. I'd gladly 'leg in' to any situation with my best mate by my side, but regardless, I certainly wasn't going to get robbed again without a scrap. I rushed into the cowshed and picked up a length of rusty iron that I'd noticed earlier. Shining my torch beam into the room, I rushed through the connecting door, swinging the iron bar, "right, you bastards, you're having it," I shouted to an empty room. There was a charged atmosphere, like static electricity, the air was almost buzzing, almost palpable. There was also a strong smell in the room, like matches and cordite, or fireworks as if someone had been lighting bonfire night bangers. The pile of tins against the wall had been knocked down and scattered over the floor, and one of the tubular steel chairs was lying on its back.

Bizarrely and most chillingly, though, there was a neat pyramid of cans stacked carefully on the tabletop. My whole body was covered with goose bumps, and the room felt freezing. This neat stack of cans was singularly the most terrifying and bizarre thing I'd ever seen in my life. My blood ran cold. An animal could have knocked the pile of cans and the chair over, but only a human could have stacked them in a neat, precise pyramid on the table. Suddenly, I realised there was something wrong with this place.

I don't remember too much about what happened next. I think I just grabbed everything and threw it onto my groundsheet, bundled it up, stumbled through the connecting door, and rammed all my gear into the top box. I pushed the bike off its stand and flicked on the ignition and the petrol. I started the engine, thankfully, first kick. I rode down the cart track with my helmet just slung on my arm and rammed open the gate with my front wheel.

I turned to look back at the house, half expecting to see something horrible chasing me, but everything looked serene and quiet.

Still shaking with fear, I rode the bike hell for leather down the road, and a few minutes later, saw the welcome streetlights of the village. The cafe wasn't open yet, but I was just relieved to be close to other living beings. I parked the bike under an ancient covered market in the square and still shaking like a leaf and freezing cold, I pulled my sleeping bag out of the top box and wrapped it around myself. I don't know what had just happened to me back at the old house, but it certainly wasn't natural. I kept racking my brains for an explanation, but I just couldn't figure out how somebody could have stacked those cans so precisely in the small amount of time I was out of the room.

The cafe opened half an hour later. Still shaken up and slightly dishevelled, I walked in and ordered coffee. I listened to the banter between the locals and the cafe owner. It sounded wonderfully normal.

I phoned Elena that evening and told her what had happened to me over the last two days. She had some quite choice words to say about the 'French *banditos*' who had robbed me, but she was mainly relieved that I hadn't been hurt. When I told her about the 'house of horrors,' she was aghast, but not surprised. She was quite cross with me, though, and she told me: "Daniel, never stay in a place like this again. Bad things can happen in these places. That's why no people live there anymore."

She seemed to find it perfectly rational that I'd had a strange, probably supernatural experience in an old, abandoned house. We resigned ourselves to the fact that I'd have to pick grapes until I could get enough money together to make the final push for Spain.

That night I stayed at a busy municipal campsite, surrounded by other tents full of noisy campers and tourists. There was a man in a tent a few yards from mine who was snoring all night and farting loudly. It was a beautiful noise, and I slept like a baby. I even had my favourite recurring dream; the one where Debbie Harry was sitting on my face.

SIXTEEN

Working My Way Back To You

ANOTHER FULL DAY of riding long straight roads, through forests that seemed to go on forever. The little bike was running sweetly at a steady forty miles per hour. After a few hours riding though, my back would start to ache, and for relief, I'd change my riding position. Sometimes I'd ride for miles without seeing any other traffic. If the roads were empty, I'd ride side-saddle or lie flat on the tank with my feet on the rear footrests to alleviate the aches and pains of sitting in one position for hours on end.

Me and Tom always used to fool around on our bikes, standing on our seats or steering with our feet. We fancied ourselves as stunt riders after being very impressed with the 'Wall of Death' at the funfair in Skeggy, especially the guy who rode the wall with his feet on the handlebars, thundering around the vertical wooden wall on an antique, girder forked, Indian motorcycle.

With the big top box on the back of the bike, I

found I could easily slide onto the pillion seat, lean against the top box, wedge my feet onto the handlebar grips, and ride for miles on the near-deserted, arrow-straight French back roads in relative comfort.

I rode past a police car in this recumbent manner. Even worse, I was smoking a cigarette through my open visor, as if I were lying on a beach rather than riding a motorbike.

The *gendarme* had parked off the road, his car hidden in the trees, in that sneaky way that traffic cops do. I didn't see him until I was nearly on top of him. I actually saw him doing a comedy double take at me, before screeching out of the pull-in, sirens blaring and lights flashing. He had a little Inspector Clouseau moustache, and he was enjoying his moment of power enormously. Comically, he walked around me and the bike several times, hands clasped behind his back, muttering and kicking the tyres. His English wasn't great, so he gave me a long and convoluted rollocking in French which I didn't understand, though he did muster enough language skills to call me a "stupid fucking English kid."

I piled on the contrition, and when he asked me what I was doing in his country, I told him about my long journey back the Spanish girl. I even showed him her picture. Thankfully, the French are a romantic race. They understand the intricacies of the *affaire de coeur,* and after hearing my story, he softened a bit. He didn't give me a ticket but told me sternly not to ride like an idiot and wished me *bonne chance* with finding my girl.

I reached the vineyards of Languedoc by late after-noon, and by the early evening, I was following directions from a small and pretty village to the farm that the German girls had recommended. I rode along a dusty track, following signs for the vineyard and knocked on the open door of quite a grand looking stone-built farmhouse. Pretty, fancy bantams and chickens pecked around the ancient flagstones in the yard. Mme Bardin, the lady who answered the door, listened patiently to my pre-rehearsed enquiry for work and told me that picking didn't start for two, maybe three, days, but I could stay at the campsite in the meantime. She pointed me to an area behind the house, where a few hundred yards away beyond the outbuildings and barns, I could see a few tents already pitched. I thanked her, rode down the field and chose a place to pitch my tent.

The campsite had a decent timber-built shower and toilet block (proper toilets but no seats) and a sink for washing clothes. This was good news. I was running out of clean things to wear. The weather had been hot, and I probably didn't smell so great.

Next door to the shower block was another building with a gas burner for cooking. There were pots and pans and a big old-fashioned fridge. Considering the campsite was free, it was a godsend. I put up my tent and rode to the village to buy food. If I were careful, my money would last me until I'd earned some wages. I wouldn't starve thanks to my German friends. I even managed to afford some cheap, strong French cigarettes. They stank like a burning privet hedge and gave me a voice like Bonnie Tyler, but they were better than nothing.

The campsite filled up over the next two days, mostly with French kids around my age, a few Germans and two English undergraduates, who were on a working holiday. There were about fifteen of us in the campsite group, and the rest of the pickers would be local people who helped with the '*Vergdange*' every year. We started picking in earnest the third day after I arrived.

People of all ages from the village joined us, from young children to eighty-year-olds. Every morning at first light we'd pile into the old Citroen 'Tube' van which the '*Vigneron*' Monsieur Bardin, used to ferry pickers to and from the fields. Each one of us was given a pair of secateurs, and we were split into gangs. Every team of a dozen or so workers had their own foreman or '*contre-maitre*,' these men were usually full-time employees of the vineyard and organised the gangs.

Each picker had a partner, and we worked either side of the vine, never directly opposite each other, but slightly staggered, so we didn't accidentally cut each other's fingers off with the secateurs. If it rained, we carried on working, and people who had them, changed into waterproofs. Thankfully, though, the weather was mostly perfect. The skies were blue, and the views from the high slopes were breath-taking.

As a rookie grape picker, the *contre-maitre* partnered me with a middle-aged Frenchman called 'Fulbert' who lived in the nearby village. He was a lot of fun, almost a caricature of a Frenchman with a constant smile, a beret, and the obligatory stub of a *Gauloises* permanently stuck in the corner of his mouth. Fulbert was liable to break out into song at any given moment. He was a real charmer with the ladies, and he made everybody laugh all day long, even though I usually didn't have a clue what he was talking about. He spoke a little English, though, and with my schoolboy French, we managed to communicate quite well. He called me 'Danny Rosbif,' which I didn't mind. I told him about my journey back to the Spanish girl, and like the *gendarme*, he'd embraced my cause with wholehearted enthusiasm. To a Frenchman from Fulbert's generation, such things as love and thwarted passion are as important as bread and wine.

When your basket was full of grapes, you shouted out on the top of your lungs, "*PANIER.*" A man would collect it and leave you with an empty basket. Mid-morning, we always stopped working for a *machon* (a chew). The French considered this a light mid-morning snack. It consisted of bread, cheese, sausage, cold meat, coffee and cold drinks, including beer if we wanted. Fulbert and I always plumped for the beer.

Mme Bardin served the food on a trestle table at the end of the rows, and we usually found some shade to sit and eat. There was always ample food for everybody, and the mood at the *machon* was cheerful and light-hearted, with people chatting in several languages. The German girl was right—the Bardins looked after their workers well.

Picking continued until around 1:00 PM, when we stopped for an hour and a half dinner break. The French pickers usually brought quite extravagant picnics and drank wine with their leisurely lunches. Fulbert would slip away and eat his lunch with a pretty widow from the village whom he had designs on, and I sat with the other kids from the campsite and ate the sandwiches I'd saved from The *Machon*. Due to the lack of funds, I'd become very frugal recently.

Picking carried on in the afternoons with radios playing and people singing along as they worked. Every other song seemed to be either Boney M or ancient French 'chanson' songs, which the older folks loved. We were in the fields for around ten hours every day, though the two breaks were long and leisurely. Despite the hard work, I was enjoying myself. When one field was picked clean, we'd move on to the next one. Sometimes it was the field next door. Sometimes it was miles away. The Bardins were the biggest producers in the area.

In the evenings, we cooked for ourselves in the campsite kitchen and we sat around the campfire when it was dark. One of the German boys had a guitar, and he loved playing Beatles songs, which reminded me of home. Everybody was friendly, and there was a holiday atmosphere in the camp. People spoke about where they were from, and where they were going, and when It was my turn, I told them my story.

They were impressed. I supposed they should be. I was probably the only transcontinental, destitute, lovelorn idiot on a moped any of them had ever met.

I passed the photo of Elena around the campfire, the one I'd taken of her on the beach in a yellow bikini. The boys reacted in the usual way according to nationality. The French boys said, "Oh, *là là*," while the German boys politely raised eyebrows and remarked, "*Schone madchen!*"

Had there been any working-class English kids like

myself present, they would have said something like, "Cor blimey! You don't get many of those to the pound," or, "Dunno what she sees in you, mate." The young English undergrads just politely said things like, "Wow! She looks charming, Daniel," and, "Crikey! What a pretty girl!"

The girls looked slightly disinterestedly at the photo but still said, "*Tres jolie*," out of politeness. A French girl called Christine, who'd been quite flirtatious for the last few days, became quite sullen when she discovered that she'd probably been wasting her time on me, but it didn't take long before the young German guitarist became her new love interest.

When I showed Elena's photo to Fulbert in the vine-yard, he clutched his heart and said, "Oh, *là là!* I come wiz you *en Espagne*, Danny. She 'as muzzer?"

I told him I hadn't met her 'muzzer' yet, but I thought her dad could be a bit of a handful.

At the end of the first week, we were paid and considering we were fed and given an excellent place to camp. The money wasn't bad—about forty-five francs a day. If the *Verdange* lasted for another week, as the *contre-maitre* told me it would, I'd have earned enough money to get me to Spain, with a bit leftover.

I went to the village to buy more nasty cigarettes, food, and batteries for my cassette player. To be honest, I was getting used to the cheap French smokes. They weren't that bad. They provided a head-spinning dose of nicotine and reminded me of my mate Byron. I posted a letter to my parents, telling them everything was fine, and I was grape picking en route to Spain for some extra cash. I never mentioned the robbery to them.

I called Elena from the village call box. I told her in one week, I'd start my journey again. Then only five hundred miles and we'd be together. Five hundred miles didn't seem so far anymore. She hadn't told her dad that I was on my way to Spain, but she planned to tell him at the weekend because Tia Pili was visiting for a couple of days, so along with her mam, Elena would have some serious back up. I imagined the situation—three tenacious, vocal Spanish women versus one poor man. He didn't stand a chance.

I sent a letter to Tom, telling him all about my adventures so far, the haunted house, the robbery, and wrecking Johnny the Bastard's truck. I asked him not to mention the gory details of the trip to my mam and told him that he should come grape picking because there were loads of horny teenage French girls to meet.

I also sent the letter to Trudy that I'd been putting off for ages. I tried to be upbeat and make the message heartfelt, but I just couldn't seem to frame the words. Everything I wrote sounded condescending and stupid. In the end, I just wrote and told her I missed her, and signed it, *Love, Fonzie xx*. She'd probably screw the letter up and toss it into the bin in the corner of her mam's kitchen. I still felt very bad about upsetting her.

When I wasn't thinking about Elena, I was thinking about Tom and Trudy. Nobody had ever made me laugh as much as those two. I missed them a lot. I'd never been apart from them for more than a few weeks in my entire life. Sometimes I found myself thinking about them and laughing out loud in a boulangerie or smirking stupidly at a petrol pump attendant.

They used to prank each other continually. Tom would sometimes think he was getting the better of his sister, but Trudy was way too clever for him.

When Tom put Holly and thistles in his sister's bed. Trudy didn't even comment, she didn't complain to her parents or make a fuss, she just kept her mouth shut. "She's doing it on purpose," Tom told me a few days later. "She's just trying to make me sweat, well it aint working, I'm on my guard every hour. Day and night."

Trudy's system worked though. The impending revenge prank started to prey on Tom's mind. He started to get nervous and jumpy. Every night he'd carefully check under his bedsheets for booby traps. He just wished she'd get it over with.

When it eventually came, Trudy's revenge was subtle, and well planned. She'd waited for more than a fortnight to pull it off.

Tom had come home drunk after a Friday night session with me and Bullshit Dave. We'd pooled our money and got smashed on cooking sherry, which you could buy by the pint from a wooden barrel in our local off licence. She'd crept into his room in the early hours and carefully emptied a quart jug of warm water into his sheets. Tom woke up in a soaking wet bed, still drunk and unsure if he'd peed the bed or not.

The next morning as he tried to smuggle his bed sheets into the washing machine, his mum caught him red handed. Tom immediately blamed his sister for the wet bedding. Sue pointed out the state he'd been in the night before, and all Tom could do was hold his hands up.

Over the breakfast table that Saturday morning, the atmosphere was a little strained.

Trudy stood up from the table and said: "Thanks Mum, breakfast was lovely, I'm off to Kim's, can't wait to see her, have a good chat, keep her up to speed with current events in the Green household". She winked and smiled at her brother as she sashayed out of the kitchen door.

Trudy's magnum opus, though, was in the spring of 1975. Tom had sent a Valentine's card to the geekiest kid in the village and signed it from his sister. He'd bragged a bit too much about the prank though, and news of it had reached Trudy's ears.

She didn't retaliate until weeks later when she set her alarm to wake her in the early hours of the morning. [This was when Trudy did her best work.] She crept out of bed, slipped into Tom's shoes, where he'd left them by the kitchen door and walked a half mile around the village, stepping into every dog turd she could find. She left the crap covered shoes where she'd found them, and slipped back into bed, happy with a job well done.

When Sue, who was always first up in the morning, came downstairs, the kitchen was filled with the all-pervading stench of dog shit. She soon traced the disgusting smell to Tom's loafers sitting on the doormat.

Tom got a huge bollocking, and he was late for school on account of spending a challenging half hour cleaning the disgusting mess from his shoes., Trudy told me the story on the school bus. I laughed until my stomach ached.

The grape harvest took another week to finish. When we'd picked the last grapes, the Bardins organised the traditional harvest feast for the workers in the '*grange aux dîmes*,' an ancient, cathedral-like barn adjacent to the farmhouse. The old building was swept clean, and trestle tables and benches were placed down the centre and covered with linen tablecloths. A large barrel of beer and crates of last season's wine and Calvados stood on side tables.

According to Fulbert, Mme Bardin's harvest feasts were legendary, and he wasn't exaggerating. We were served bowls of soup with fresh bread, charcuterie of every description, huge steaks and fruit pies with cream. An accordion band from the village played, and the older folks danced to the traditional French music. We all drank too much wine, as you're inclined to when it's free, and woke up with banging headaches the next morning.

M. Bardin told us we were welcome to stay on the site for a few days longer. Some people were stopping a while before heading to Bordeaux for the later picking season, but I was anxious to head to Spain and my girl, as soon as I could. I packed my gear and checked the bike over. After the robbery, I had very few tools left, and I was desperate to buy at least a plug spanner, a screwdriver and an adjustable spanner. Fulbert had told me there was a motorcycle shop in a little town about ten miles south, in the direction I was heading, so I planned to call in there en-route.

I said my farewells to the people who were staying on longer at the campsite, I'd made some good friends amongst this crowd. Nowadays I always seemed to be saying goodbye to people. I rode up the field to the farmhouse, stopped at the kitchen door and said "merci au revoir" to Madame Bardin. She handed me a bag of croissants for the road and wished me, "*Bon voyage.*"

Grape picking had been a blessing for me. I'd had a good time and earned enough cash to keep me travelling. Now all that separated me from my girlfriend was about a four- or five-day ride, a vast, mountain range and an overprotective father. I had a warm, optimistic feeling in my guts that it would all be 'plain sailing' from now on. But sometimes I could be a proper 'Hampton wick' as my old cockney grandad would have said.

SEVENTEEN

Bent Legs and Gravel Rash

THE LITTLE ROAD wound quite steeply down the valley with a sheer rock face on my right-hand side where stunted pines clung on grimly. On my left was a steep, wooded hillside, edged by a low crude bank of rocks, earth, and small trees to discourage drivers from driving over the edge. The road was shady and quiet, and occasionally there were tantalising glimpses through the trees of a pretty ancient looking town a few hundred feet below. I was enjoying the ride down the valley. The sweeping downhill switchback bends were a lot of fun. I remember noticing a pick-up truck in my handlebar mirror, coming down the hill about a hundred yards behind me, just before I banked into the next switchback bend.

The White Renault 4 van, coming up the hill rounded the hairpin on the wrong side of the road, and I braked hard. The driver slammed on his brakes much too late and tried to steer back to his own side of the road. I had no choice, though—either hit the van square on or ride into the jagged rocky hillside on my right.

My front wheel hit the Renault bumper with a sickening crunch, and I was catapulted onto the bonnet and over the roof. I hit the ground hard on the other side of the van and continued travelling, sliding, and rolling along the tarmac for twenty feet or so until I slammed headfirst in a crumpled heap on the other side of the road. Without the earth and rock bank to stop me, I'd have fallen several hundred feet down the steep wooded hillside, I probably wouldn't have survived. I'd banged my head quite badly on the rocks, my helmet surely saved my life, but I was stunned all the same. I remember a lot of shouting and confusion. My head was spinning, and the impact with the ground had winded me.

A small, barrel-chested man with a grey beard and a boxer's nose appeared at my side and started talking rapidly in French. I didn't understand him.

In my dazed state, I stupidly asked him: "Are you Tom Bombadil, or David Bellamy?" He looked a bit like them both.

He replied in English with a thick French accent, "No, *mon ami*. I am Conrad Chastain, and you need the doctor."

He unbuckled my crash helmet and very carefully eased it off my head. Meanwhile, a boy who looked about my age appeared and started tying a rag tightly around my leg like a tourniquet. I looked down and saw my jeans, ripped to shreds, and a long, open gaping gash on my right leg, which was bleeding heavily. The strange thing was, I couldn't feel any pain. I suddenly felt sick, turned my head away and started throwing up. I tried to sit up to see my bike, but it was on the other side of the Renault and out of view.

I asked the man where it was, and he told me not to worry. They'd take care of it for me.

I heard voices shouting angrily in French, and then the white Renault van drove away.

I didn't remember much more about the crash. I guess I was a bit concussed from the bang to my head. The man and the boy helped me into the pick-up truck, where they propped me up between them on the bench seat. I remember the pain starting in my gashed leg, my left arm, knees, elbows, hip, ankles, and shoulder where I'd made contact with the road. Where leather and denim had ripped, and my skin had ground away on the tarmac. My head was starting to ache, and I felt sick again.

The next thing I recall is a doctor in a white lab coat, stethoscope around his neck, shining a light into my eyes, and then watching him and feeling strangely remote as he injected me and stitched up the wound in my leg while a nurse cleaned the gravel out of my grated limbs. They must have given me something for the pain, and I must have slept for ages because when I woke up, strong morning sunlight was streaming through the window. I looked around and took in my surroundings.

I was in a small room, white painted with a strong hospital smell of antiseptic in the air. Every joint in my body ached. I felt like I'd been run over by a train. A nurse came into the room and asked me how I was feeling. I struggled to find the words in French to describe my aches and pains, so I just said, "merde," and she laughed. Half an hour later, the doctor who'd stitched my leg came in and politely asked me some questions in English. He looked at the wound on my leg, shone his torch in my eyes and seemed satisfied that I was going to live.

I asked him when I could leave, and he replied, "Monsieur Chastain would come for me later, and meanwhile I should rest."

The small, round, cheery nurse brought me coffee and toast and chatted to me in French. I didn't understand much, but she was nice company, and kind in the way that nurses are when you're feeling alone and confused. Later she cleaned and changed the dressings on my gravel-rash. The lint bandages had stuck to the wounds. It was excruciating. I asked her where my clothes were, but she just shrugged and smiled.

Around midday M. Chastain arrived with some clothes from my top box. He was an upbeat and jolly chap. He helped me to get dressed and, with his aid, I hobbled outside to his pick-up truck, and struggled into the cab. He seemed like a nice fellow, and he told me to call him Conrad.

My Bell Star crash hat and wrecked leather jacket were on the front bench seat of the truck. I picked up the helmet to inspect the damage. It was a ruin. There was a deep, nasty scrape down the side, the visor had shattered, and there was a massive dent in the fibreglass where my head had hit the rocks. I shuddered when I saw it.

"Bon casque," said Conrad, pointing at the dent.

"Oui," I agreed, "bon casque."

My jacket had fared little better, the leather had ground away and ripped on the left sleeve where my skin had made contact with the road. It was a second hand 'Lewis leather' jacket with a 'Fifty-Nine Club' badge sewn to the arm. An old rocker from the village had sold it to me. I loved it. It was a crying shame, but I guess it had done its job and saved my skin.

Well, some of it anyway.

I was really pissed off about my white 'Bell Star,' though. I'd saved up for months and months to buy it, picking potatoes in the holidays and working for Phil at weekends while I was still at school. I'd had it since I was fourteen. It was costly. Evel Knievel had one though, so it was worth every penny.

Suddenly panicking, I searched the breast pocket of my leather. With relief, I found the photo of Elena, still intact. I looked at the dog-eared picture for the thousandth time and passed it to Conrad.

"My girl in Spain"

He wolf-whistled through his teeth, and said: "You go to *Espagne*?"

I told him the story. He was surprised. "From England to Spain on such a little moto. What do we do for a pretty girl, eh?"

He told me that the doctor said I had to rest and not bend my leg for at least a week, or the wound would probably open. I asked him if there was a camping place nearby, he replied, "No, you stay at my house. Please, we have space."

Panicking suddenly, I asked him where my bike was, and he told me it was at his place of work. He had a small engineering business, and he and his son had taken it there.

I told him I'd like to see it and he drove to the edge of town where a small industrial building, maybe two thousand square feet or so, stood in a yard. Breezeblock walls and a corrugated tin roof. Inside, it was noisy and hot. A radio was playing, and several men, including the boy who'd put the tourniquet on my leg, were working at lathes, presses and milling machines. The boy stopped working, waved and walked towards us, he held out his hand, and we shook. Conrad introduced us, "Daniel, this is my son, Vincent."

Pointing at my injured leg, I thanked him for his help the previous day.

"*De rien*," he replied, smiling, and motioned me to follow him to the back of the workshop. I limped on with some help from Conrad.

My bike was standing on its stand with the forks removed. Vincent showed me the bent fork leg stanchions which were lying on a bench nearby. He explained that they could straighten them with the huge and ancient, heavy-duty fly press that stood against the wall. Conrad told me he'd taken the front hub to the moto shop in town and they were lacing a new rim to it, fitting new bearings and a tyre.

I held my hands up and said, "Conrad, I'm sorry, but I don't have enough money to pay for all this work and the new parts, and I think the man who ran into me has disappeared."

Conrad shook his head emphatically and said loudly, "No! The idiot baker who nearly killed you is paying for everything. He drinks too much, and then he drives. He's a fool. If you want, Daniel, we can call the police. The choice is for you. We see the crash and his crazy driving." Then he added slightly awkwardly, "He is my wife's brother. He's a good man when he isn't drinking wine, but he has a problem." He lifted an imaginary wine glass to his lips in explanation.

Despite the battering that I'd taken from his brother-in-law, I felt a bit sorry for this kind little man who still reminded me of my favourite character from *The Hobbit*.

"No, I don't want the police, Conrad. I only want to get to Spain and my girl. If you can help me fix my bike, that would be enough, and I'd be grateful," I told him.

The painkillers that the nurse had given me before I'd left the little cottage hospital were wearing off. I was starting to ache like crazy again, and the gravel rash was hurting like hell. Conrad drove me back to town to a big house set back from the main street at the end of a leafy driveway. His wife, smiling, slender and a couple of inches taller than her husband, met us at the door, Conrad introduced us and showed me into the big, beautiful old building. Madame Chastain told me to call her Colette, and made a fuss of me, plumping cushions, and finding a footstool for my injured leg. Unlike her husband, she didn't speak a lot of English, but my O level French was still paying dividends.

To their seven-year-old daughter, Sophie, I was a curiosity. She just peeped around the door and laughed at me. Once again, my bad luck had been repaid with good luck and kindness. I must have a guardian angel.

The Chastains were a noisy, entertaining family, and very soon, I felt at home in their house. That first evening they fed me, gave me the painkillers the doctor had prescribed, and then put me to bed in a spare room on the ground floor. I went out like a light and woke up the next morning feeling a lot better. My body had taken a hammering when I landed on the tarmac. Every joint had been shocked and jarred, but twenty-four hours later, the aches and pains were subsiding.

Over a breakfast of hot croissants and coffee in the cheery kitchen overlooking a beautiful garden, Conrad recalled my comment after the accident and laughed, "Daniel, do I really look like Tom Bombadil?"

He told me he was an avid fan of English literature. The house was full of books—a lot of Shakespeare, Kipling, and Dickens. And he'd read *The Hobbit*, my childhood favourite. I apologised and told him it was a compliment. Tom Bombadil was my favourite Tolkien character. Colette told me I must phone my family in England and tell them I was okay.

After breakfast, I called my mam on the phone in the hallway. I told her the bike had broken down, and I was staying with some friends. It wasn't a lie. It just wasn't the whole story.

"I told you that you wouldn't get to Spain on a moped, Daniel. Now perhaps you'll see sense and come home."

I just told her not to worry because my friends were helping me to fix the bike, and I was okay and still heading for Spain and Elena. Lately, I'd started to feel guilty and a bit sorry for my mam. I knew she'd be worrying herself sick, and I knew she loved having her family around her. I'd decided I was going to make it up to her one day.

Later, a nurse called at the house to change the dressings on my injuries and check for infection. She visited for the next few days until my wounds started to heal. That evening, I called my girlfriend and told her: "don't worry, but I've had a crash. A drunken French baker hit me with his van. The bike got wrecked, and I got some cuts and bruises and banged my head, but I have some friends, and they're helping me."

I told her my fork legs were bent, but they thought they could straighten them for me. For a few seconds, there was silence on the other end of the line as she absorbed and deciphered my words. Then all hell broke loose.

"*MADRE MIA*! HE BEND YOUR LEGS. *CABRON, BORRACHO*!" Then an uninterrupted volley of Spanish cursing that I didn't understand, and then, "Don't worry. I love you if your legs are bent. I love you with no legs. Where are you? I'll come to you now."

She was quite distraught, crying and very cross, she said quite a lot of unkind things about the French as a race and drunken bakers in general. Jesus, my girlfriend was a spitfire! Five feet, three inches of unbridled Spanish fury. If the baker were in the same room as her, she'd have probably ripped his throat out. I made a mental note never to upset her too much, she could probably be dangerous.

Eventually, I got a word in edgeways and managed to explain that it was my 'fork legs' *de mi* moto, not my 'poor legs' that were bent. Thankfully, she calmed down enough to laugh at the misunderstanding. I told her I had to wait until my wounds had healed enough to ride, and then I was only three or four days away from her. She wanted to ask her dad to drive to France to rescue me, but that would have been awful. I begged her not to do that. I was going to have to face her father soon, and I needed to get to Spain under my own steam.

I stayed with the Chastains for another seven days. My wounds were healing well, and the swelling in my gashed leg was going down. I wrote to Tom and Trudy and told them all about the crash, but I asked them not to mention it to my mam and dad.

I spent the days in the house and garden. Sophie was my usual companion. She was funny. She read storybooks to me in French, and we played board games and *pétanque* on the lawn while I taught her English words. I also had free reign with Conrad's superb library. I read *Plain Tales from the Hills* by Rudyard Kipling and became a lifelong fan of the writer. In the evenings, I sat with the family and played cards, or we talked late into the night over a few glasses of wine. They were nice people.

As soon as I could walk a little easier, I went to the factory with Vincent and Conrad to help put my bike back together. The fork legs had straightened well in the press. We rebuilt them with new seals, and they worked fine. The front-wheel looked good with a new flanged alloy rim and tyre, and the boys in the factory had done a pretty good job of straightening out the front mudguard and welding up the brackets for me. After a week, I went back to the little hospital with Conrad, and a nurse removed my stitches. I was planning to leave the next day, and that evening I phoned Elena and told her I'd be back on the road in the morning, we figured we were less than a week apart now. She was as excited as I was.

Most of my good clothes had been either stolen when my bike was taken or ruined in the crash. My helmet was a wreck but still wearable, and I'd attempted to sew my leather jacket back together. I must have looked like a bit of a tramp, but I was going to be with my girl soon, and I didn't really give a damn about anything else. Vincent had given me some half-decent jeans to wear, so at least my arse wouldn't be hanging out of my trousers.

The Chastains were taking me out for dinner on my last night. That afternoon, there was a knock at their front door. Colette showed a tall, slightly gaunt man into the kitchen, where I was sitting at the table playing games with Sophie. She introduced me to her brother, Andre, the drunken baker who'd nearly killed me a week before. He was desperately and genuinely sorry, and he apologised profusely. Collete assured me that Andre had sworn never to drink and drive again since the accident.

He carried a large cardboard carton in from his van and placed it on the kitchen table. Inside the box was a brand-new Bell Star helmet, my size. It was bright, shiny orange with a new visor. There were also two pairs of new Levis and a brand new 'Lewis style leather jacket. I couldn't believe it. It was wonderful. I shook Andre's hand warmly and thanked him. I might have been limping, but at least I wasn't going to meet my girlfriend looking like a down and out.

Conrad told me his brother-in-law had driven all the way to Perpignan to find the Bell helmet in my size. Before he left, Andre shook my hand again. He wished me *bonne chance*, *bon voyage*, and handed me an envelope, which I expected contained a 'get well soon' card. I opened the envelope after he'd left and found five hundred francs inside. It was a small fortune to me (around sixty pounds). I told Conrad he should give it back to his brother-in-law for me, but he told me to keep the money because I deserved it and I'd need it too.

I didn't argue with him. I knew I'd been 'paid off' by the baker. But the Chastains had been so lovely, and I shuddered to think what would've happened if Conrad and Vincent hadn't been following me down the hill in their pick-up.

The next morning, I loaded the bike and said my farewells and *merci beaucoups* to the family. I'd miss them, and I promised to keep in touch and let them know when I arrived in Albarracin. I kicked up the bike, slightly awkwardly with my left foot, and rode off down the drive and out of the pretty bustling little market town.

My Fizzy felt great. No wobbles, the forks were damping well, and the new front rim and tyre felt fine. I was struggling a bit, riding, still sore from my injuries, but if I took it steady, I'd be okay. On the mountain road, I passed the place where I'd collided with the baker's van. My bloodstains were still visible on the tarmac. I looked over the drop on my right and thanked my lucky stars I hadn't slid over the edge and fell down the rock-strewn slope.

It felt good to be heading south again. I wanted to cross the border into Spain near a place called La Jonquera. Conrad and Colette told me to be careful if I stopped there. Apparently, it had a dodgy reputation.

EIGHTEEN

Shanty Town

THE ROAD to Narbonne was a long, arduous, uphill ride through beautiful scenery. At first, the landscape was surreal, with perfect green valleys and trees that looked like manicured topiary in the grounds of an English stately home, or the scenery painted on my mam's prized Clarice Cliffe vase—a wedding present from my gran and grandad.

I had to stop often to straighten my leg, which was still hurting. It took me a long day to travel the next ninety miles of mainly uphill road with stunning views over breath-taking valleys; always heading uphill, one switchback bend after another. As I got higher, hundred-foot-high spiral columns of huge, scary, pterodactyl-like Egyptian vultures rode the mountain thermals, looking for dead meat below. I didn't want to fall off here.

High up, the landscape finally plateaued out, and vineyards started to appear, signs by the roadside advertising *Minervois* and *Corbieres*. Some fields had been picked clean of grapes; some were still being gathered. I cast a professional eye over the work in progress, the workers straightened their backs and looked up at the sound of my noisy little bike on the lonely mountain road.

There were solitary, dusty stone houses on the route with faded pastel ghost signs painted on the walls facing the road: Ricard, Dubonnet, and Michelin. I passed through remote villages and stopped at a petrol station with a single glass globed pump straight out of the 1950s.

This late in the season there were few campsites open, and the light was fading fast.

On the outskirts of a tiny village, I stopped and asked an old man who was digging potatoes in his garden if there was anywhere to camp nearby. He told me, "*Non*," and then pointed at the small lawn adjacent to his vegetable plot. He showed me an outside tap behind the house and an ancient wooden *'thunderbox'* toilet in a small shed. There were squares of newspaper strung together and hanging from a hook on the wall.

He asked me where I'd ridden from, and I told him England. He stood and stared at me for a while, shaking his head and repeating the word *'Angleterre.'* Then he went and fetched his tiny grey-haired wife, who also stared at me in wonder, as if I was an escaped lunatic or a museum exhibit.

I was grateful, though, and I thanked him and asked him, "How much?" But he wouldn't take any money. He just shrugged and showed me where I could leave my bike.

In the fading light, I pitched my tent and unpacked my stove and cooking kit from my top box. Before I could start cooking, the old man called me from the kitchen door and invited me inside, where his wife had set a place at the kitchen table for me.

Dinner was the newly dug potatoes and rabbit stew with homemade bread. It was delicious. Noticing my limping gait, the old man asked if I was hurt. Using Franglais, with a little bit of Spanish (which they seemed to understand), I told them my story. The old lady smiled the biggest smile and reached over the table to squeeze her husband's hand; I think she was happy to be helping 'star-crossed lovers.'

It was tough sleeping on the hard ground with my injuries still quite raw. The Chastains' big, comfortable bed had spoiled me. I cushioned my still painful gravel-rashed hips with rolled up clothes and eventually slept okay.

The next morning, I packed my kit and said '*au revoir*' to the old couple. I tried to give them some money, but they wouldn't accept a single franc from me.

They stood by their garden gate and waved me off. I was heading for an ancient little border town.

La Perthus was a strange no-man's-land with one foot in Spain and the other in France. Full of 'tat' shops and cheap booze and tobacco stores. The streets were crowded with people, hauling cut-price cigarettes and monster-sized bottles of Pastis back to their cars.

That afternoon, a lazy border guard hardly glanced at my papers as I rode out of France and into post-

Franco Spain, with my parents' words still ringing in my ears.

"You can't ride to Spain on a moped, Daniel!"

I felt victorious, happy, and slightly emotional. Now I was standing on the same soil as Elena. I headed for nearby La Jonquera and changed all my francs for pesetas at a bank downtown that advertised '*Cambio de dinero*' on a neon sign in the window. Then I rode up the street to find some food.

The bar was nearly empty, two policemen were sitting at the counter, eating tapas and drinking cloudy '*Pastis.*' They eyed me suspiciously as I walked in. Keeping an eye on my bike through the window, I ordered a foot-long *bocadillo queso* from the glass chiller on the countertop and a can of Coke. I paid and walked out before the cops started asking me questions. I needn't have worried too much, though. La Jonquera was full of strange and curious people, and besides, the Guardia Civil eyed everybody in Spain with suspicion, so I guess a kid on a moped didn't attract a lot of attention.

I limped back out into the sunshine to find a girl sitting on my bike, leaning casually up against the top box. She was about my age I guessed. Pretty, shoulder-length brown hair, long-legged, wearing a very short suede skirt and jacket. She was smoking a cigarette, head back, blowing the smoke into the sky. She smiled when she saw me and said *"Hola Guapo."* It took me a moment or two before I realised, she was a 'working girl.' I'd seen a lot of girls hanging around the lorry parks and bars on my way into La Jonquera and even some girls working from the lay-bys a mile out of town.

Her name was Martine, she was from Toulouse, and she spoke French, Spanish, and English, seemingly fluently. I shared my sandwich and Cola with her and told her about my journey and my girl. She flirted with me a bit and said Elena was lucky. I told her I thought I was the lucky one. She was very sweet though, and I wondered why a smart girl who could speak three languages was 'on the game'. She told me her Mamon was an alcoholic, Toulous was a dump, and she'd never known her dad. She said she was only doing this until she'd saved enough money to go to London where her sister lived and worked in 'Kings Cross'. [I didn't ask her what her sister did for a living.]

She walked to a nearby pharmacy to buy me painkillers because I'd ran out, and I was still finding it painful to walk. She told me all about her life in this weird, wild west frontier town in the east. She went back into the bar and bought two bottles of Spanish beer, the first I'd had since the holiday in Lloret. We sat at a little metal table in the sunshine, drank the cold beer, smoked, talked and laughed like any other teenagers in the world, even though one of us was a prostitute and the other a limping teenage runaway. Before I left, she planted a passionate kiss on my neck and asked me if I wanted to fuck for free. I was sixteen, horny, and lonely, but I declined her tempting offer. There was only one girl on my mind.

I rode out of 'Dodge City' before it started getting dark. I looked back to see her waving from the cafe car park. She looked small and vulnerable like a child, and I felt desperately sorry and worried for her. I wondered for the next forty years how her life had been. I hoped things turned out good for her.

That night I stayed at a small campsite in a place somewhere between La Jonquera and Figueres. I rang Elena from a callbox in the village bar. She picked up the phone in the campsite reception and I shouted into the mouthpiece, "*ESTOY EN ESPAÑA.*" [I'm in Spain]

The old men sat drinking at the nearby table looked up, and one of them raised his eyes and shouted to me, "*SI, CLARO.*" [Yes, obviously]

Elana and I were both laughing out loud, elated and excited. It was hard to believe that in a few days we'd be together again.

In the morning, I headed for the coast where the land was flatter, and the riding got easier, fewer gradients, and mostly downhill anyway. I passed through Lloret with butterflies of nostalgia in my stomach. This was where it had all started ten weeks ago when I'd seen a vision sitting at a bar table. It seemed like years ago. I stopped in town just long enough to mail postcards to Tom and Trudy, my mam, dad, and Jim. To my family, I wrote,

I'M IN SPAIN! Back in Lloret. I made it! You can ride to Spain on a moped, mam! (Though it's not easy.) I should be with Elena by the time you get this postcard. I'll phone you. Love Danny.

I could imagine my mam picking up the postcard from the doormat in our hallway and reading it. It made me feel a little bit sad, I hoped she could be happy for me.

That night I stopped a few miles north of Barcelona at a campsite behind a busy roadhouse. There were just a few other campers on the site, Spanish families taking late summer breaks. I had a couple of beers and some tapas in the bar. It was Saturday night, and the locals didn't appear until after 10:30 PM, when they turned up en masse and didn't leave until the birds were singing. I liked the Spanish way of socialising. Especially 'out in the sticks' Unbothered by licensing hours, they drank without urgency. I watched them in the bar. The local *guardia* was sitting amongst them, drinking and joking, dressed in his weekend clothes, but still wearing a pistol in a holster on his belt.

The next morning, I headed west towards Lleida following the dotted lines on the map that Elena and I had drawn weeks before in my hotel room in Lloret. I remembered us both lying on our stomachs on my bed with the map spread out in front of us. The plans we had made were almost like a dream at the time, but now we'd nearly made them a reality.

The landscape became hilly again with less vegetation and bleak rocky outcrops on the horizons. The weather was still warm, though the nights and mornings were getting cooler. The temperature suited my bike better, though, and I didn't have to stop and clean the spark plug so often.

I rode non-stop for more than a hundred and twenty miles. There were no campsites so I wild camped behind a bar near Lleida. I was only about two hundred miles from my girl now. I phoned her from the bar and told her I'd be with her sometime, late tomorrow night. She said she'd be waiting at the *'gasolinera* on the edge of town. I could hear the excitement in her voice. I don't think either of us could quite believe it.

NINETEEN

Radar Love

I GOT up at first light with an excited, nervous feeling in my stomach. Today I was going to see my girl. She was more than 'my girl.' She was my everything. I'd spent every waking hour thinking about her since the first time I'd seen her, petite and perfect, sitting outside of the tackiest bar on the Costa Brava. As I packed my tent down and loaded the bike, I reminisced about leaving home all those weeks before, pushing my bike up the street and slipping out of my village at dawn. I thought about Tom and Trudy back in Church Lane, still snoring away in their beds. Tom and Phil would be getting up for work in an hour or so, and Sue would soon be yelling up the stairs at her daughter, "Trudy, get out of bed, you lazy little mare!"

My mam would be getting up soon. She'd be making Jim's sandwiches for work, while my dad would be brewing the tea. I missed those morning sounds and smells. The rattle of spoons in teacups. My mam singing along to the radio in our kitchen. The smells of toast, coffee, and bacon. My dad's first cigarette and coughing fit of the day.

I'd been on the road for two months, and I'd started to feel that I didn't belong anywhere. If everything went to plan, I'd be with Elena tonight, after that, God knows what we'd do. To be honest, I didn't care. I just so desperately wanted her in my arms.

I sat in the bar and ordered coffee, fried eggs, and a bag of churros for the road. My map was spread out on the table in front of me. The route didn't look too bad, and I hoped to cover the two hundred miles to Albarracin in one day, though I knew it was going to be one of my longest single rides of the whole trip.

I headed for a town called Alcaniz, which would be about the halfway point, and the first eighty miles went by without any problems. The little bike buzzed along happily as if it knew it was on the final furlong. The rugged landscape gave way to rich farmland, and the day heated up quickly after the morning chill. I rode past vast fields of late maize, wheat, and barley. It was still being harvested, the combines kicking up clouds of dust which hung over the dry landscape in clouds.

I suffered my first puncture of the trip. I couldn't complain, nearly sixteen hundred miles until my rear tyre released its 'last gasp' of Leicestershire air into the warm Spanish midday atmosphere, via a small tear in the inner tube caused by a thorn. I was about ten miles from Alcaniz. I had a puncture repair kit and an adjustable spanner, but no pump or tyre levers. I had no choice but to start pushing the bike and hope that I came across a village, farm, or garage soon.

I pushed uphill for around a mile. It was hard going, and my leg soon began to hurt. I coasted down the other side of the hill for a few hundred yards but then had to start pushing uphill again. There was no sign of life as far as the eye could see, no roadhouse, no garage, nothing but tarmac, corn, and sky. There was very little traffic on the road, and I had no choice but to carry on shoving the bike. Eventually, though, a tractor and trailer came over the brow of the hill, and I stuck my thumb out for a ride. The old boy driving the ancient Fordson tractor stopped and gave me a hand lifting my Fizzy onto the trailer. I sat on the bike to keep it upright while we rattled down the road. He dropped me off in the deserted square of a tiny village a few miles off the main road, pointed to a pair of corrugated tin clad doors and said "*Aqui el mecanico.*" I thanked him, and he trundled off down the dusty street.

The mechanic's shop was closed, doors bolted, and there was no reply when I knocked. The sleepy little village seemed empty except for me, and a scruffy dog who was lying asleep (or dead) on a bench by the ornate waterless fountain in the centre of the run-down spaghetti western plaza. I heard a murmur of voices from behind a door nearby and limped off to investigate.

The door had a rainbow-coloured plastic fly screen over it and painted above in whitewash was the single word 'Cafe.' I imagined Mexican banditos, gold toothed, grinning, and ready to rob me of every penny. With more than a little trepidation, I walked into the dark smoky interior of the tiny bar. The room fell silent, and the half-dozen male customers looked up from their lunchtime drinks and conversations at the stranger who'd just walked through their bar room door. If I'd been wearing a poncho and a six-gun, I wouldn't have looked out of place.

After a few seconds, though, the conversations resumed, and one or two of the men nodded at me and mumbled, "*Buenos dias.*"

The old lady behind the bar was quite friendly. She smiled and said, "*Hola.*"

I asked her if I could have a beer and, clutching my phrasebook, I told her I needed a mechanic. "*Necesito el mecanico, por favor.*"

She looked at the clock on the wall and replied, but I couldn't understand her.

I looked at her blankly and shrugged. "*Yo soy ingles.*"

She simplified her answer for me, and spoke slowly: "*Mecanico siesta, aquí tarde.*" (Later.)

I drank my beer in the dark little bar, happy to be out of the sun, listening to the conversations of the customers and trying in vain to understand the tommy-gun speed dialogue.

I was impatient to get back on the road though, so I went and took the wheel out of the bike.

I couldn't do any more without help and some tools, so I went and sat on the bench with my fellow vagrant—a scruffy dog and a scruffy kid together. He stirred, opened an eye, and looked at me as if to say: "You waiting as well, mate?" I tickled him behind his scabby ears, we shared some churros and then dozed off in the sun.

206

Nearly two hours later, a young fellow wearing an oily baseball cap and overalls walked into the square, glancing at me and my bike, and nodding as he walked by. Guessing this was the *mecanico*, I followed him into the bar, where he asked for: "*Mi vitaminas, por favor,*". *Vitaminas* was a large glass of brandy and ice. This was my first encounter with the 'daytime' drinking habits of the Iberian working male. In Spain, it seemed standard practice to wake from an afternoon nap and jump start your metabolism with a shot of strong alcohol, a nerve-jangling 'cafe solo,' or both, before going to the office or workshop. It was a sensible routine if you asked me. I liked this country more and more.

The old lady introduced me to Francisco the *mecanico*, and I asked him if I could borrow a pump and some tyre levers. He seemed to understand, and I followed him out into the square where he opened his workshop doors and fired up a creaky old compressor. Twenty minutes later, the puncture was fixed and the *mecanico*, seeing me struggling to 'tread' the tyre onto the rim with my injured leg, helped me to refit it. He refused payment for his help, so I followed him back into the bar and ordered another large *vitamina* for him. Francisco insisted that I stay for another drink, so I swigged a cold beer, told my story for the hundredth time, thanked him again and said my adioses to the bandits in the bar. I gave old Scabby ears, who was still dozing on his bench, a pat on the head and the last churro from my top box.

It was after 6:00 PM when I left the village. In a couple of hours, the sun would be sinking over the horizon. My butterfly filled stomach churning with the prospect of seeing my girl. I headed off south towards my destiny.

I rode hard and as fast as I could. The little bike kept up a steady forty-five miles per hour on the mainly flat roads. It was half-past one in the morning, and a fine cold drizzly rain was falling when I passed the ancient city of Teruel and headed west off the highway onto a small road over deserted flat farmland. There was no light whatsoever—no moon, just pitch blackness either side of my feeble six-volt headlamp beam. The road didn't deviate. It was as straight as an arrow for miles and miles. Until after what seemed an age, there was a bend in the road, and I headed through a low mountain pass and into a valley, where the temperature rose by a couple of degrees and the rain eased. I stopped at a small village and looked at my wristwatch. It was after two in the morning. I should only be half an hour from Albarracin now. I didn't expect Elena to be waiting for me at this late hour, she'd probably been waiting since the end of her shift on reception at 7:30, but I wasn't too upset. I'd find her in the morning, or maybe I could ride into town, find the campsite and pitch my tent there.

There was an enormous black sheer cliff face to the right-hand side of the road, and my exhaust note was ricocheting pleasingly off the hard stone. On my left, I sensed a drop, that was probably the river that ran through the gorge.

The butterflies in my stomach were going crazy. I just couldn't believe I was so close to her.

After several miles of dark, lonely riding, I saw a faint light up ahead, maybe a mile away. Just an occasional glimpse through the trees, as the twisty little road meandered with the river. Finally, the route straightened out, and I saw the light from the petrol station that my girl had mentioned. I opened the throttle, intending to ride straight past the garage and head towards the town, but when I was a couple of hundred yards away, I saw a small figure standing under the illuminated sign.

My heart started beating like a jackhammer. She was there, waiting for me. She knew I'd get there. From miles away, she'd heard the faint, distant sound of my bike's noisy exhaust note echoing off the rock faces as I made my way up the dark valley road.

She was already running to me as I leaned the bike against the wall, limped towards her, and pulled of my helmet. As petite as she was, she hit me with the velocity of a small charging bull and very nearly knocked me over.

Shouting my name, she threw her arms around my neck. I held her very tightly and buried my face in her hair. I'd been longing for this moment for nearly three months. It felt incredible, wonderful, beautiful. I breathed deeply and inhaled the scent of her skin. The Elena-shaped hole that I'd had in my guts for months was gone, instantly and miraculously, as if someone had inserted the missing piece of a jigsaw puzzle. I'd been battered and bruised, robbed, haunted, and soaked to the skin dozens of times, but I'd have turned the bike around and done it all again in an instance for this amazing girl.

She pushed me away briefly by my shoulders and looked me in the face, touching my cheeks with her fingertips as if she couldn't believe I was real. She said that I'd lost too much weight, then she ran her hands gently down my legs, just to satisfy herself that they weren't bent. In both English and Spanish, she told me in no uncertain terms that she loved me and that she always would. We held each other and kissed so hard that it almost hurt. Her face was wet with tears, or maybe the tears were mine. I couldn't really tell.

She pulled something from her pocket and handed it to me. Our hands were shaking with emotion. It was a small box. I opened it. It contained a silver Saint Christopher medallion on a chain. In the light from the neon gas station sign I saw engraved on the back our initials in a heart.

"*Feliz cumpleaños mi amor,*" she said.

It was my seventeenth birthday, and I hadn't even noticed.

TWENTY

Sweet and Dandy

ELENA'S UNCLE Blas had a *finca*, he grew olives and kept sheep for making cheese. His cheese was amongst the best in Aragon, and it was served in some of the best restaurants in Spain. He also had a small *cortijo* in the hills on the edge of town. His niece had begged him to let me stay there in exchange for some labour. I was understandably slightly suspicious of old farm buildings after my strange experience in France, but this place was different. Although ancient, it was cosy and comfortable. Like most *cortijos*, it was designed as a temporary home from home for harvest times. Elena and her siblings had stayed there as children when they'd helped pick the olives or almonds, camping out and cooking for themselves on the old cast iron stove, loving the independence.

Uncle Blas was the brother of Elena's mam and Tia Pili, a small, wiry, no-nonsense man of few words, but as straight as a die. The first work I did for him was to help him extend the building where they produced the cheese. We dug the foundations, laid the blocks and built the pan-tiled lean-to roof. I did a super neat job of the block work, and he was very impressed.

During my first six months in Spain, Blas and I became good friends. His wife Maria was the yin to his yang; she was as loud as he was quiet, a coiled spring of energy, always laughing, always joking. She cooked the best food I'd ever eaten in my life, even better than my mam's, and she never looked in a cookery book, retaining generations of recipes in her head. They seemed the most unlikely couple: the quiet, slightly taciturn man, and the loud eccentric little woman—funnily enough, though, they fitted together like a pot and a lid.

Over the next few months, along with Elena, they taught me to speak basic Spanish, and Blas taught me to drive in his battered-but-beautiful old Mercedes.

I got to see my girlfriend every day, and we walked through her hometown when we had time together, holding hands while she introduced me to people as her *novio ingles*. I revelled in the jealous looks I got from the local boys.

The few initial encounters I'd had with Elena's parents had been pretty good. Her mam and I got on fine, but her dad still treated me with guarded suspicion. I think he realised I was there to stay, though.

When he saw the work, I'd done on Blas's extension, he asked me to help him to build the new shower block that he'd planned for the campsite. We sat one evening in early December at the kitchen table, looking at drawings and discussing the design of the new building. Slowly we became friends.

I moved out of the Cortijo when the weather turned cold and lodged in one of the chalets on the campsite, taking my meals with the family every evening, after working on the shower block or helping Blas back on the farm.

Elena and I were married a year later in the autumn of 1978, a week after my eighteenth birthday. My parents and the Greens flew out for the wedding.

We rode the mile from the church, back to the campsite on the Fizzy, cleaned and polished, but still a bit battle scarred. The plug fouled up a hundred yards from the campsite, and the engine stopped dead. Laughing like idiots, we pushed the bike the last hundred yards up the hill. The wonderful little bike had carried our hopes and dreams for more than sixteen hundred miles. She'd been overloaded, crashed, and abused. She couldn't quite make the last few yards. We forgave her, though.

The large *banquete de bodas* at the campsite was held outside. The weather was still mild and the few remaining late season campers on the site were invited to join the party, along with more than a hundred guests. Everybody in town seemed to be there; the butcher, the baker and the guy that delivered the *butano*. I looked around at the faces, my family and friends from England, and then I looked at my wonderful girl. For a moment I couldn't quite believe we'd done it.

It was the first time I'd seen my parents in over a year. They'd loved Elena the moment they met her. My dad, sharp-eyed as ever, asked me how the tank got dented on my bike and I had to come clean and tell my parents about the accident. While I was about it, I told them about being robbed as well as some of the other gory details of my long and eventful journey to Spain.

My dad looked at my beautiful wife and said, "Well, I think she was worth it, son."

My mam just hugged me and said, "You silly bugger. You could have killed yourself."

It was Saturday, the seventh of October 1978. I was sitting beside the only girl I'd ever want. It was the best day of my life so far.

Epilogue

TRUDY HAD BEEN ill eighteen months earlier, but she'd beaten the disease and was thankfully in remission. Elena and I had been back to the UK to visit her recently, and she was doing well. She was as happy and optimistic as ever with her husband and two daughters making a fuss of her. She'd recently celebrated the birth of her first grandchild.

Over the years, we'd all stayed close. Tom and Trudy, along with their partners and kids, had visited us often over the years. Our children had become good friends. We always came home at Christmas time to visit my folks and to see the Greens.

Phil had died a few years earlier, and my dad had followed him soon after. My mam was still alive but quite frail. She and Sue were still the closest of friends, and since Dad and Phil had died, Sue and my mam had been constant companions.

For our whole lives Tom and I had spoken several times a week on the phone, or more recently via email.

I knew there was something wrong the moment I picked up the phone. I knew Tom as well as I knew myself. His voice cracked with emotion as he told me that Trudy had relapsed, and I should come to England if I wanted to say goodbye to her. My legs almost buckled beneath me at the news. I dropped everything and booked the first available flight back to the UK.

Her blithe spirit left this earth as I was somewhere over the Bay of Biscay, staring dully out of the cabin window and willing the plane to fly faster. I arrived to find a family broken to pieces. Tom was devastated. He told me his little sister had been brave and stoic to the end. She'd died in the arms of the man she loved with her daughters by her bedside. When Tom had told her, I was on the way, she'd smiled through the morphine, squeezed his hand, and said, "Good old Fonzie."

Tom and I walked over the park. Nothing much had changed, though the old wooden pavilion where Trudy had celebrated her sixteenth birthday more than forty years ago had gone, and in its place, a smart brick-built replacement stood. People were walking their dogs and kids were playing on the swings and slides.

The fair hadn't been to the village for more than twenty years, since the new housing estate had been built next to the park. Tom said the people in the new houses had complained about the noise, and the parish council had refused to allow funfairs on the park anymore, breaking a century-old tradition with the sweep of a ballpoint pen and a nondescript note in the meeting minutes. Instead, a small group of local showmen with soulless, vinyl bouncy castles and a few juvenile rides were allowed a four-day pitch in the summer holidays as long as the music was silenced by seven PM.

We stood in the exact spot in the field where Joe Parker's beautiful old Waltzer was pitched all those years ago. I closed my eyes, and I could hear the roar of the wheels on the tracks as the platforms thundered around the hills and valleys on the Waltzer's never-ending journey. I could hear the screams of the passengers as Sim and Byron spun the cars. I could hear the thumping beat and sub-bass notes of Dave and Ansel Collins's "Double Barrel," and I could almost smell the hot dogs, crushed grass, and Dodgem sparks.

I'd missed Trudy. I should have come back earlier. I never got to say goodbye to her, and I felt almost inconsolably wretched. Tom had apologised to me for not letting me know sooner how ill she'd been. But I knew he'd been in denial, hoping and praying, willing her to get well.

In a way, though, it seemed right. She wouldn't have wanted me to see her like that. Not Trudy. Nothing ever beat her.

I'd been spared the agony of seeing my childhood friend on her deathbed, and in a strange way, I was almost grateful for that. The little '*duende*,' my teenage tormentor and sparring partner whom I'd loved and cared for like a sister—it only seems like yesterday when the impish, infant Saxon had fired crab apples at Mrs Taylor's tea stall from the church tower.

When I think of Trudy now, it's always May 1977, and she's in a Waltzer car. She and her best friend Kim are holding onto each other for dear life as Sim spins the car like crazy. "Let Your Yeah Be Yeah" by the Pioneers is pumping out of the PA system. Trudy's hair is flying behind her, and she's laughing out loud for the sheer joy of living. It's a cherished, longed-for and special moment, frozen in time from my past.

I'm looking at her from the other side of the car, where Tom and I are sitting. She's so pretty, and her brown eyes are shining, reflecting the lights from hundreds of coloured bulbs.

Reading my mind, Tom said, "She loved the Waltzer, didn't she mate?"

I turned to look at him, my lifelong best mate, big, handsome and amiable, the spitting image of his dad. Tears were running down his face—mine too. He put his arm around me and squeezed my shoulder. "C'mon, mate. Let's go and have a pint.

The End

Printed in Great Britain
by Amazon

50891351R00123